AN UNBROKEN PROMISE

By

Kathryn Wood

Published by

Garner Benge Group
Des Moines, Iowa

Ornella,

I'm so glad you've been a friend for all these years. You've always been a positive presence.

Kathryn Wood
October 5, 2013

An Unbroken Promise

By

Kathryn Wood

Published by Garner Benge Group, L.L.C.
Des Moines, Iowa

First printing: November, 2012

ISBN-10: 1480152242
ISBN-13 978-1480152243

Printed in the United States of America

Dedication

To my heroes:

Ed, my son, and Laura, my daughter. I watch them, I listen, I study their words and behavior, and I learn.

To one of the best friends I've ever known, a friend who came into my life when I needed him most and left when his assignment to me was finished. He walked by my side, seldom let me out of his sight, growled menacingly at strangers (until I showed approval of them), and slept on the floor by my bed every night. He seemed to know what I wanted or needed without any words from me, often, I think, carrying my burdens as his own. Others have come into my life and others will appear, but there will never be another friend like him.

Thank You

Thank you, Mary Boardman, for mid-wifing the birth of this book. Without you, the words would still be lying on the lined pages of my spiral notebook and in the mystery spaces of my computer. I appreciate you.

Table of Contents

Part I
The Dog in the Gazebo

Part III
A Promise Kept

PART I

The Dog in the Gazebo

Chapter One

The Stranger

The afternoon sun had gathered unexpected warmth for an early April day, a day warmer than most April days, signaling the end of winter of 2003 and promising great expectations for many sunny days to follow. Popcorn clouds decorated the sky as Leah walked to the gazebo with a cup of hot lemon tea, a pen and journal, a book to read, and a padded cushion for the wicker chaise lounge. A friend had suggested to her that writing her thoughts and feelings each day would be good therapy, a healing process to expend her sadness. She had found in that process a means to record her path to recovery. That move forward wasn't noticeable to her if she looked for it daily, but months later, when she reread those journal pages, she was surprised how her feelings had mellowed. Later, glimpses into those pages hinted to her that she wanted to live again.

Stepping into the rounded gazebo, she felt a warm, southern breeze playing under its roof. Leah moved the chaise lounge into the shade and covered its splintery boards with the orange poppy-flowered cushion. She set the steaming tea on the floor and straddled her short legs across the lounge's seat. She took a moment to enjoy the peace that always abided in this open, white structure.

As she laid her head against the back of the cushion, she allowed another memory to drift to the front of her mind. She closed her eyes and smiled at the remembrance of the anniversary card Logan had given her six years earlier. She had opened the card, read its sentimental pledge of love from him, and then unfolded the torn page from the farmers' magazine. The glossy page had displayed a picture of a small, white gazebo with benches built inside its short walls. The note on the card declared the gazebo would be built as soon as crops were harvested. He had promised they could spend evenings there, even into their old age if that's what she wanted.

Leah opened her eyes and picked up her book, setting aside the journaling for now. She hadn't allowed herself yet to read the light romances that she had loved in the past. She couldn't go there just yet. Instead, she had chosen a book about Jackie Kennedy Onassis. That Camelot era had ended the year she was born, but history had persevered in telling the stories of a charismatic, though unfaithful, president and his steadfast wife. Leah was always intrigued by whatever substance could have been so enmeshed in a woman that made her always exhibit such an unobtrusive persona to the public.

Somewhere in the years of Jack Kennedy's courtship of Jackie Bouvier, Leah drifted off into a scarce, but peaceful sleep. The fallen book lay open on her chest, and her arm dropped beside the chaise. With a start she awoke to feel a moist tongue lapping her hand for attention. Sitting bolt upright, she looked anxiously at the large dog beside her. Indifferently, he returned her gaze.

The two earnestly measured each other. Leah observed a mature animal who appeared to be mostly German shepherd with short legs that indicated the intrusion of one or more other breeds. He was black and brown, but the serene face was golden, that color blending down into the dark neck. A wonderfully thick tail was black and matted with unruly knots. The hips and shoulders over the short legs spoke of power. His ears were erect, but the brown (or were they black?) eyes locked her in his gaze. Leah was cautious around strange dogs, but she felt no unease with this magnificent if unorthodox animal.

He in turn studied a countenance that was a window to sadness. Blonde hair lightly encircled a face that provided carriage to brown eyes, eyes that hadn't wrinkled with laughter for several months. In just an hour the sunshine this April day had brought a warm pink to her pale cheeks.

"Well, good afternoon, my good man." She leaned forward and said, "Aren't you the handsome one! And what brings you calling to my gazebo? Are you out for a stroll in the neighborhood?" She laughed at her nonsense, but continued, "Is this a business call of some kind, or are you just being sociable? Where do you live because I've never seen you around here? Never."

Leah rubbed her hand over his shaggy head and down his neck.

"No sign of a collar. Someone just drop you off? That can't be. You're a handsome fella." Leah was rubbing her hand along his back and down his short black and tan legs. I don't know what your blood lines are, but you must be German shepherd with a cross of Golden Lab. And those short legs? I can't imagine where you got them, but you are a very good looking boy."

Leah's running dialogue gave her his story. Truth or fiction, it was her story, and her self-imposed questions and answers completed all the information she needed to know except, of course, where did he live and did he belong to someone.

She swung her leg over to sit on the side of the chaise and looked at the interloper. He backed from her and continued to watch her. The fallen books were retrieved as she picked up the empty cup.

She then suggested, "Come up to the house, and I'll see what I have for you to eat. Then I'm going to make some calls, and we'll see where you came from." But not to get his hopes up, in case he did understand her, she admonished, "And don't think you're sticking around here because I have other things to do than take care of a wandering mongrel like you."

The stranger wagged his gnarly tail and followed her as she walked up the incline to the house. At the edge of the patio he found a spot on an old rug which lay in disarray on the sunny side of the large, vintage, but still naked lilac bush. From the refrigerator Leah stole a leftover hot dog which she broke up and put into an aluminum pie tin, adding as an afterthought a crumbled slice of wheat bread and leftover cold green beans.

"Not particularly what the vet ordered," she mused, *"but a hungry dog might go for it."*

Five or six phone calls to the neighbors yielded no information about her new friend, where he belonged or to whom. One neighbor had seen a large dog that morning, trotting along the gravel road, but other than that…nothing.

Leah opened the back door and, as she had expected, found that the feast she had prepared for him had been devoured. The tail thumped when he heard the screen door open. She filled the wrinkled, aluminum pan with cold water from the garden hose and placed it on the ground before him.

"Well, let's just consider that you might stay around, and I'm not saying you can, what would I call you?"

He lapped up the water, and if he were listening at all, gave no indication. The pan was soon empty, and he eagerly peered upward. Watching her adoringly, he wagged his tail so hard he wagged his haunches.

She laughed, "Oh, you'd be a hard one to dismiss, wouldn't you? Well for now, I'll just call you Stranger. If you should stick around, and that's a big strong 'if', we'll talk about a better name later."

She stroked him gently under his eyes and walked back into the house.

PART II

Logan's Promise

Chapter Two

The Marine

The cracks in the sidewalk were uneven, intermixing Leah's frustration at her small town Iowa existence with her appreciation of the dangers in the broken cement.

She wanted to enjoy her glum, to savor the despair. This Sunday afternoon of 1984 brought no break in the desolate routine of the end-of-semester break from Iowa University. After three relaxing weeks, the beginning of this fourth week was bordering on the dull side. It was much like many other weeks in her home town of Glendale, and she was eager to return to school to finish her senior year.

Somewhere in the turn of the world there must have occurred a whisper of a season without the dreary cold, but Leah sensed no warmth in this January afternoon, nor were there any suspicions of sunshine. With her hands thrust deep into her pockets, she pulled her navy pea-coat tighter to her chest. The soft, angora stocking cap Grams had knitted for her was snug and comforting. She made no observation of the mounds of dirty snow which had been pushed aside by the city snowplows. Her small town was a myriad of grays and browns, colors that lent themselves to her darkening, depressed mood.

Leah looked up to see a maroon Ford pacing her. She saw the round face of her friend Sarah Cummings grinning at her from the passenger's seat of the car which belonged to Sarah's current boyfriend, Dan Mason. Leah knew him as the young man who had broken the hearts of several of her girlfriends. He was the dream of just about every young lady in their town and the bane to every one of their dads.

The window rolled down, and Sarah called, "Hey, Little Lady Leah. Need a ride? Come on and hop in."

Sarah was a friend of long standing though Leah hadn't seen her since last summer. Leah opened the passenger door to the coupe and climbed in behind Sarah. She saw she was sharing the back seat with Logan Cummings, Sarah's brother. Finishing Glendale High two years before Leah, he had graduated from Iowa State University and then late this summer had enlisted in the Marines. Apparently he was now home on leave.

Sarah was ready with unneeded introductions.

"Leah, have you met my brother, Logan? He just got in Friday evening from Camp Pendleton. Our boy's on his way to becoming a Marine, a studly Leatherneck."

Leah turned to look at him more closely. Obviously, he could be identified as a Marine by his jar head haircut which was showing some evidence of growth. *"Good Lord,"* she thought. *"These guys are going into the service to do God only-knows-what, and then the military brands them with this ridiculous haircut. Otherwise,"* she admitted to herself, *"he looks pretty darned good."*

Leah was turning the image of Logan Cummings over in her mind. Delving into her memory, she remembered a young man who had made a record for himself as a football quarterback his junior and senior years and then had gone to state both of those years as a wrestler. Both memories brought pictures of a strong, trim young man, but now he was even more sculptured…and now he was studying her. She had pulled her long, blonde hair away from her face, and she knew the stocking cap allowed only the ends to show. So much for style.

"How long do you get to stay? Do you like the Marines?" she asked. "Is it hard to be away from home? I mean it has to be different from college, doesn't it? Where do you think you'll go after you leave here?" Leah heard her voice going on and on and on. She thought to herself, *"Just shut up, why don't you? You sound like a third grader."*

"I should be here a full two weeks. I have to head back in another week," Logan replied with a grin. "Basic training could be tough, but being a farm boy from Iowa helps prepare you. Baling hay is always good prep. And, no, I don't get homesick. Did all that when I went to State. Well, maybe I did suffer a bit there for a day or two." Logan stopped, reflected, and then proceeded. "You're kept so busy, though, that you really don't get much of a chance to be homesick, anyway. Now the part about 'Do I like being a Marine?' Yeah, I guess I do. I think I'll like it even better now that I'm through basic. Makes you feel kind'a proud. No, it does make you damn proud."

Logan's answers were not at all patronizing. He was delighting in looking at Leah and was amused at her discomfort. He studied the petite frame and the face with the brown eyes. The walk on the brisk January day had colored her cheeks red, which was a break for her; it concealed some of her fluster.

"Leah, we're going to a movie tonight." Sarah was turning from the front seat and directing conversation back in their direction. "Why don't you go with? And, Logan, you're not doing anything tonight. Why don't you pick up Leah? Dan has to take me back home so I can check in with the folks and get a different sweater since I spilt chili dog on this one. Then, Logan, you can pick up Leah when she's ready. How about that?"

Leah was overwhelmed. What had she just experienced? *"Is this what happens when a tornado comes bearing down on you?"* she mused.

"Now let me get this straight," she was asking. "You're kind of roping this new Marine into taking me to a movie tonight. And I imagine he's as overwhelmed at this as I am."

She turned to Logan and said, "I'm sorry. I didn't know all this was happening." In a gesture of mock desperation, she held out her hands to him, palms up, "But she's your sister. Do you have any say in any of this?"

Logan laughed. "My little sister missed her calling. She talks about going to college after she graduates, but she would make a perfect drill sergeant. Now this is how you get things done. Actually, I think she has a good idea, and if she hadn't said something, I know I would have. I'm not very good, though, at the asking part so this is much easier."

Logan looked steadily at her face which had reddened again. "Would you like to go to the movie with me tonight? I'll beat it back to the house and get the folks' Buick since I don't have wheels now. I can pick you up by 6:30 if that's okay with you."

Leah had not dated much. There just hadn't been enough time. When she examined the discourse that had just transpired, she decided that that's what this was.

"A date. How did this happen?"

"I'll let the folks know," she replied. "I don't have anything else planned. I can be ready by 6:30. It'll be fun." *"Sheesh. Sounds like I'm going just because I don't have anything else to do"* she thought. She gave an imagined slap to her forehead.

With his three passengers Dave circled the Main Street loop of their small town before they decided they should be on their way. He stopped in front of her house, and Leah wrestled herself free from the back of the two-door Ford.

"I'll see you in about an hour or so."

Walking to the house, she felt like she had run a race, a long race. She was emotionally exhausted, but she was excited about a date with Logan Cummings. *"I feel like I'm in a daze, and I don't even know how all this came about, but I'm pretty sure I'm glad it did. A date. With Logan Cummings. Nice."*

Chapter Three

The Confrontation

Leah stepped onto the back deck of the two-story white frame house and sat down a minute in one of the green Adirondack lawn chairs. She removed her stocking cap and leaned against the hard back of the chair, one of several chairs that were usually tucked away in the back of the garage at this time of year. Closing her eyes, she recalled a time when she had welcomed the attention of Logan Cummings. She remembered a time four years earlier, another afternoon at AJ's when she was just a senior in high school.

That particular afternoon Leah had anticipated seeing Ryan James, also a senior, but, alas, a senior from Mission Falls, a small town of comparable size as Glendale and laid out on the plains twenty-two miles to the west. The town fathers and the school board had decided years earlier not to consolidate with the Glendale school district, and the school had for several years maintained its independence to exist as its own entity. However, eight years ago the school had been ordered by state public education leaders to unite with one of its neighboring towns, and so Mission Falls had merged with its neighbor further west. It was now a part of the Four Corner School District. Subsequently, Glendale residents viewed the schools that composed that district as the birthing ground of young men who would eventually be interred in some penal institution some time or another. From the same visionaries it was assumed that all those young ladies would complete the family cycle and merely continue those blood lines of those august citizens already inhabiting that town.

The Glendale Consolidated School District, which consisted of Glendale and two other small school systems, competed each year in all athletic events with the Four Corner School District. They found themselves in the same conference, and if Glendale lost every game in the football or basketball season, they still considered the season to be

a success if they beat the Four Corner School District.

Remembering the events of that afternoon, Leah recalled looking with anticipation from time to time at the door of AJ's. Sometimes on Sunday afternoons a car with its maximum load of teenage boys would drive over from Mission Falls. Their town, too, lacked an abundance of activities for the young people. Driving the twenty two miles to view the pulchritude of young ladies in a neighboring burg might be worth the trip. Ryan James found that ride to be necessary in order that he might have a chance to see Leah. They had met at the swimming pool the summer before. Mission Falls boasted the only public swimming pool in the surrounding area, and it was one place the youth from neighboring towns could meet and become acquainted without the stigma of competition of school events. Ryan had immediately been attracted to Leah's smile and loved her penchant to tease. She was not put off when he countered her teasing in return. There were phone calls, and he tried to see her whenever he made the trip to Glendale.

In spite of the attraction he had felt for Leah, theirs was not a dating relationship. Ryan was well accepted by his male peers, and senior and junior girls enjoyed his sense of humor and air of rascality. In fact, his parents and older brother often jabbed him about the many phone calls from those same girls, those lengthy calls which intruded into their evening hours of television. Ryan appreciated the attention of the young ladies, and although Leah was not one of the callers, she did receive his calls with what he perceived as a certain amount of enthusiasm. Those phone calls were usually limited to an hour by her parents, but those hours did speed by quickly.

Now he was in Glendale and was hoping she might be at AJ's. He parallel parked with a deft turn of the front wheels and glided backwards into a slot in front of the restaurant, the hub of the local young peoples' activities. The four doors of his Chevy Impala flew open almost simultaneously. Three boys bailed from the front seat and four more stepped quickly from the back. In one mass they entered AJ's. Ryan unzipped his black letter jacket with the scarlet sleeves. His dark hair was longer, as was the style, though not shoulder length. He wasn't quite six feet tall, but he was tall enough to survey the room without appearing to be searching. His dark-lashed eyes found Leah in the corner with several of her girlfriends.

Ryan strode to the table, scooted a chair close to Leah, and lightly placed his leather jacket over its top. He turned the chair and straddled its seat, then leaned his arms across its back. Resting his chin on his arms, he sat quietly for a minute. Obviously, his presence was no surprise to Leah or the other girls. He waited, and in a moment she disengaged herself from conversation and turned to him.

Leah smiled and said, "Hello, Ryan. I'm glad you could make it to our little metropolis today. I hope you got your heater fixed in your car. But then, you may not have really needed it with all that hot air from you Mission Falls boys." Her teasing was charming and inviting.

"If it had been thirty degrees below zero, and if not one word was spoken on the way over here, it would still have been worth it just to be sitting here next to you," Ryan replied, looking steadily into her eyes. Not even a smile.

Leah giggled. "Oh, you're really good."

Ryan's face was familiar to the other occupants of the table, and introductions weren't necessary. Conversation continued with banter about football, with emphasis expressed on how Glendale would surely beat the Four Corner School team in the next week. Ryan could handle a lot of teasing, but after a while, the bantering did become a little irritating. It was one of him against a table of six and sometimes seven. But, after all, he was on their turf. As Ryan defended his team's coaching and the skills of his teammates, a second young man approached their table. Noting his long, brown hair tied in a band at the nape of his neck and the jeans which rode low on his hips, Ryan came to a negative, preliminary conclusion. The intruder seemed to be known to the others in the circle, and Leah introduced him to Ryan only as Mike.

When one of her friends moved to another table, Mike sat in the vacated chair on the other side of Leah. For a few minutes he solely controlled her attention. Their conversation was between them, but Ryan heard Mike ask Leah if he could take her home when they were all ready to leave. Her response was unintelligible to him. In deeper conversation with Mike, Leah had turned her back slightly to Ryan. He felt himself being ignored by the others at the table. The burner on his temper was still simmering on low from the razzing about his coach and teammates, but he reminded himself these were comments made from a group of backers who hadn't had a winning team in at least seven years…probably longer. Now, to irritate him even further, he was watching a young man move in, talking to Leah when he himself had been talking to her.

Ryan looked around AJ's and found that his Mission Falls buddies were all in conversations with various girls. He felt like the outsider…not his usual place. Feeling some discomfort, he stood, turned his chair around and sat down again, this time leaning very lightly against its back.

Mike stood and took his car keys from his pocket. He stepped away from the table and brushed against Ryan's chair, knocking the black letter jacket to the floor. A look of disdain was given to Ryan but no apology.

The young man from Mission Falls stood up, sliding his own chair backwards. He could feel the slow burn rising to a boil.

"What's the rush?" he asked quietly. He continued, speaking with some authority, "You knocked my coat off the chair. Now, do you mind picking it up?"

Mike dismissed Ryan with a look and turned to Leah.

"When you're ready, I'll give you a ride home if you'd like."

Ryan felt his face and neck becoming hot. In a quiet voice which he felt would have made his coach proud, he said again, "You just knocked my coat to the floor, and I just had it cleaned. Pick it up."

Mike took a few seconds then and actually observed Ryan.

"Aren't you from Mission Falls? Maybe you and your pals would find your time better spent in your own little one-horse town," Mike responded, rising to Ryan's challenge. "Why don't you take that little Chevy of yours and head it back down the road? I think you'll fit in better there."

Ryan did not consider himself to be a trouble seeker, but he would not step back from a fight. He was rational to the point that he knew he should retreat from the situation being played out in front of him, but he was just irritated enough that he knew he couldn't make that move. He knew it would feel good to slug this "twit".

Ryan stooped to pick up his own coat. He stepped to the side of his chair and away from Leah.

"I've not seen Nasty from anyone in your town before…that is not until now. I think if you want me out of town, you'll have to take on that job yourself."

Barely had the words spelled from his lips when Ryan saw the right fist flash towards his face. Stepping back, he avoided the blow, but the wild swing caught Leah to the side of her face. She fell onto the table and then slumped to the floor. Ryan pushed Mike away and at the same time leaned to his side, hoping to catch Leah before she fell from her chair. Before he could catch the petite figure, a lean figure loomed between the two. Ryan caught a glimpse of Mike as that young man leaned in again to throw another punch, this time to the midsection. Now off balance, Ryan could not dodge the blow. The punch knocked the air from him, and he fell to the floor, gasping for breath. From the corner of his eye, he could see a young man attending to Leah and helping her back into her seat. For now, he had his own mess to attend. As he tried to stand, he felt the hard kick of Mike's boot in his stomach.

Ryan lost awareness of the action that occurred next. He learned later the young man who tackled Mike was Logan Cummings. Straddling him, Logan rolled Mike to his stomach and pinned his arms behind his back. By this time, AJ's cook appeared and declared that all action was over for the day and that all the Mission Falls boys would be better off to drive west. Mike was allowed to stand up and grab his leather jacket. He was then told to leave, posthaste.

Leah pressed the "rewind" button in her mind. She had seen Ryan on occasion after that, but he had become a distant friend. After high school she had enrolled at Iowa University. Ryan had attended a university in Arizona on a baseball scholarship. She assumed he was probably finishing there as she was at Iowa. Funny...she couldn't even remember what happened to Mike. He had never been anyone she wanted to know better. He appeared in Glendale from time to time when he visited his mother and step dad but had not mixed anymore with the crowd at AJ's.

Chapter Four

Meeting the Parents

Dating was a new game to Leah. She had dated two boys at various times in high school, but it was exciting to meet someone new. And this someone new was "an older man." And a Marine at that. *"Hmmmm, what will Dad say about that?"*

She sat down at the round, oak kitchen table. Traditional Sunday evening meal was usually soup and leftovers, usually cold chicken from Sunday dinner. Tonight was potato soup. Her favorite. Her older brother Paul wasn't yet home from his Sunday afternoon job. Jim, her younger brother, in the hopes of feeding that growing boy's appetite, had just emerged from his room and stepped away from his efforts to master his guitar. He was committed to the thing. Another good reason for her to leave the house, although his time limit with the twang machine would expire in a half hour. Then the family would again know some peace.

"Mom, I have a date tonight, sort of, with Sarah's brother, Logan. He's home a couple of weeks from basic training, and Sarah sort of fixed us up to go to the movie. He'll pick me up at 6:30."

"Logan Cummings?" Leah's dad questioned as he crumbled crackers into his potato soup. "He should be finished at State, shouldn't he? I'd think he's been out a couple of years now. And he's in the service? What's this young man like?"

Leah took a deep breath and thought to herself, *"He knows the Cummings family. Must be the paternal thing kicking in."*

Aloud she responded, "You've seen him, Dad. And I know you know Sarah. She graduated a year after I did, and we sang and danced in Swing Choir."

"Yes, that tells me about Sarah, but it doesn't tell me anything about Logan. Now tell me about him," her dad continued.

"There's not much to tell. I didn't see him that much before he graduated because I didn't have any classes with him. He took ag classes." Leah squirmed not because she was uneasy about her answers, but because she even had to supply answers. *"Why the inquisition?"* she wondered. *"Paul wouldn't have to supply a bunch of answers."* And Mom wasn't saying anything. Just Dad.

"Like I said, he's only going to be here until the end of next week. It's just a movie. And if we really get reckless….hey, maybe put our feet up on the seats." Cute. But her sarcasm was lost on him. *"Good thing I'm going back to school,"* she thought. *"I really don't need this."*

"Guess I can't make much of a problem out of that, can I? Just be home early, Missy, and that's not early tomorrow morning." So there. Pointe returned.

Leah finished her soup, picked up a piece of cold chicken, then took her dishes to the sink. Looking at the big, round kitchen clock, she noticed she hadn't much time to change and do anything with her hair. The cap that was needed that afternoon had done a number on her hair, and she didn't have much time to mess with it. Fortunately, it wasn't loaded with spray or styling gel so she could put a wave at the tips with a curling iron.

Standing in front of the bathroom sink, hot curling iron in one hand, Leah picked at her eyebrows with the other. She studied the light brown brows and dark lashes. Nothing's ever perfect. She wished the brows weren't quite so thick, but better thick than hardly a line at all. At least she could tweeze any fine hairs that wandered astray, but at the moment, they were lying in an arched line and were behaving themselves. And that was good. She didn't have the time to mess now anyway.

Hair slightly curled and fluffed, Leah chose a soft pink sweater and pulled on clean jeans. Nikes were still the shoes for the day. A wisp of a Jovan fragrance and a pink lipstick. Such was the dress attire for a date to a movie in a small town. And it was 6:30.

"Ahhhh, and there's the doorbell." This was not one of those "Honk and I'll be out" dates. That would never happen anyway, not only from her dad's standards, but Leah's either. She hurried down the hall from her bedroom, but the front door was eagerly being opened by her brother, Jim. Of course. He'd have to meet him first.

Jim had immediately immersed himself in dialogue with the young Marine.

"Hi, I'm Jim, Leah's brother. You taking my sister to the movie tonight? She's been primping for you."

"Sheesh," Leah glared. "Come on in, Logan, so you can meet my family. But then it looks as though you've already met my nemesis, Jim. This is my mom, Grace, and

my dad, Ned Weeks. I think your folks probably know Dad from the lumber yard."

Mom had come into the living room from the kitchen.

"It's nice to meet you, Logan."

Dad, coming in from the deck, greeted him. "Logan, nice to meet you. Leah says you're in the Marines. I must say, it's a pleasure to meet another military man… and a Marine at that." He welcomed his daughter's date with a hand shake, and then asked, "How long is your leave? Actually, I was a Marine myself. Guess I still am. Always a Marine. I spent a year or there abouts in 'Nam." He was silent, and then continued. "Not a good place to be."

"I just finished basic, so I'll be heading back in a week. I'm hoping I'll get to see some of the world," Logan responded.

Leah grabbed her pea-coat and put it on in the hallway, not wanting the fuss of anyone helping her. She grabbed her small clutch purse and her mittens. She certainly didn't want to wrestle with the cap again. Smiling at Logan, she said, "Well, I guess we can go if you're ready."

Logan opened the door and stepped back. Leah walked out onto the porch and down the steps with Logan close behind. He opened the car door for her, and then he was behind the wheel. "Ummmm. Classy car," she said.

"Well, like I said this afternoon, this is my folks' Buick," he commented as he backed out the drive. "Dad said he thought it would be a good idea for me to sell mine when I went into the Marine's because it would just depreciate while I was gone, and Sarah didn't think she wanted to drive my Chevy. Not sporty enough, so Dad bought her a used car more to her taste."

Leah fastened her seat belt and leaned back into the cushion of the seat. She had to admit, it was easy talking to this young man. *"Funny. Wonder why I never noticed him before. Guess he's always been around. Maybe a person has to be out of your sight for a while for you to take a long, hard look at him again."*

Chapter Five

First Date

Movie in a small town on a Sunday night. It could be a mundane event or, for some, it could be the social event of the week. Although Leah wasn't into sci-fi flicks, the movie "Enemy Mine" had touched her. Popcorn was fresh and warm and just buttery enough. Logan even knew the secret formula of adding Milk Duds to the box. But if that didn't complete a perfect Sunday evening, sitting beside him in the theatre did. No hand holding, not even an arm around the back of her chair. She felt peaceful and happy to be seated near him.

In the dark nucleus of the theatre, Leah could discreetly study him from the corner of her eye. He looked comfortable again in civilian togs, and he was sporting an Iowa State cardinal and gold sweater. Carrying heavy bags of feed and seed and lifting bales of hay on his dad's farm had shaped a stocky but lean and muscular frame. Several months training in a Marine boot camp had even more defined that appearance, and as she remembered him, he had always sported an Iowa, generic butch cut. The Marine clip was growing again.

Leah couldn't see them now, but studying his face later as she talked with him, she found that his eyes were brown and were framed by the blackest lashes. And lying in the depths of those eyes was a source of a great gentleness.

Leah and Logan walked quietly to his car. Although there had been no significant temperature change since that afternoon, Leah did not feel the chill that she had experienced earlier. She had never at any time felt any sense of danger in her town of Glendale, but even if she were walking on a darkened street in a dangerous part of a huge metropolis, she knew she would feel as safe as she did now, walking beside this self-confident Marine.

Logan had parked the family car on a side street several blocks from the theatre. Being assured by Leah that she didn't mind, and in fact relished the stroll to the movie, he had made his decision to park away from the heavier traffic on the main street. Now as they approached his dad's tan Buick sedan, both lifted their heads as they heard the sound of a racing car coming toward them. This was a side street with barely room for two cars side by side. Parallel parking was allowed on one side, but the street was designated as a one-way thoroughfare. It was not designed for a vehicle speeding as this one was. Instead of the car slowing, the engine appeared to be accelerating.

In an instant Leah saw a small, white animal run into the street. She screamed. In less than a second the driver braked, but even if his action had been timelier, the speed of the auto would not have allowed it to stop.

A second scream, but it was not Leah's. This was the terrible sound of pain. Then the horrible scream of death. Leah's hands flew to her mouth. She tried to stifle a further scream from her own person, but there was no sound there. The huge lump in her chest and throat would have strangled any cry that screamed to escape.

The red sports car with the glass mufflers braked and slowed, but only for a second. Then the tires squealed, and the car with its passengers was gone.

Leah stood paralyzed. Logan had been standing beside her, ready to open the car's passenger door. Now he was gone. Frozen, Leah watched as Logan ran to the still, now quiet, little dog. She watched as he knelt over the small animal.

Slowly, Leah walked the twenty or so feet to them. She stood quietly, unable to speak. Her eyes filled with tears as she watched Logan gently touch the little dog. He spoke quietly to it, but she saw that the dog did not hear him. After a moment, Logan unzipped his wind breaker, took it off, and spread it on the ground near the dog. He picked up the little animal, placed it on his jacket, and wrapped it in it. Holding the wet and now red bundle in his arms, he stood and walked to the car. Nothing was said. As he unlocked and then opened the trunk, even through the hazy light of the street lamp directly above them, Leah could see the moistness gathering at the corners of his eyes.

Both were quiet until after he had started the car and they had left their parking pace. After a few minutes, Logan said quietly, "You know, they say kids raised on a farm get use to seeing death. We lose farm animals and pets, and they say we should get so that death doesn't bother us, but that's not true. I mean that's really not true. I don't think I'll ever become that immune to death. How can anyone ever become that callous?"

*   *   *   *   *   *

Logan drove the four blocks to The Pit Stop. Having a beer and dividing a small pizza would ordinarily have served as the leisurely end to a first date. Closure at the Pit Stop allowed for the continuation of dialogue and also gave those who were out that evening a chance to see who was dating whom, who composed the new couples, and what couples had broken up.

This evening Logan found no close or available parking spots. Instead of stopping in front of the young adults' bar, Logan drove on.

"If you don't mind, I could do without the chatter of a crowd of people right now. Do you care?" Logan queried. "I think I need some quiet time. That okay?"

"It isn't a matter of mind reading, I think, but you couldn't have hit my mood any better. I just can't get that horrible scene out of my mind. If you're into a drive out to Chariton River Bluffs, I'd like to ride along. I think I'd like to walk along the top of the bluffs." As she spoke, Leah was thinking that such an invitation could have been taken on a totally different flavor. Not so. Her mood was absolutely innocent of ulterior motives, and she felt confident that Logan was aware of that.

The ride to the bluffs above the Chariton River was quiet. Instead of listening to the country music of Johnny Cash or current music of Fleetwood Mac or ABBA as they normally would, Logan had inserted a CD of Celtic music. The sounds of the lilting flutes and haunting voice of an unacknowledged Irish singer lent themselves to the mood of sadness that was purveyed in the car. Neither person made an attempt at conversation; instead, both were reliving the events that had transpired.

Logan parked his parents' car on a gravel lane near the walking path. "I don't think we'll probably walk too long since I don't have a jacket now, but let's at least get some fresh air. I think that will do us both some good."

Logan started towards the passenger's door, but Leah was already out when he arrived there. Grinning now, she apologized, "Sorry, I haven't learned yet to allow someone to open a door for me. Give me time."

Logan smiled his response. "Guess I'll have to move a little faster."

Leah pushed her gloved hands into the pockets of her navy pea-coat and strode ahead of Logan on the walking path. Although the entrance to the rural park was well lit, darkness reigned on the walking trail. She walked slowly and moved to the side of the path so Logan could walk beside her. Although the afternoon had been dreary and overcast, now the clouds had left the sky, and a near-full moon was evident. Away from the shadows of the trees, they had no trouble seeing the path. They walked at first in silence.

Leah said softly, "Do you think someone will be missing him?"

"He wasn't wearing a collar," Logan replied. "There are apartments above the stores on that street, but I can't imagine pets being allowed up there. Of course, what do I know? If he did belong to someone there, what would be best? To wonder if your pet were still alive somewhere or finding it dead there in the street in a pool of blood?"

"Have you had pets before, Logan?" Leah asked.

"You don't live on a farm and not have pets. Most of them live outdoors." Logan walked slowly to match Leah's shorter steps. He spoke thoughtfully. "The cats usually make their home in the barns, and we always had dog houses for the dogs. If a calf or lamb were orphaned or rejected by its mother, we would usually make a pet of it. Mom usually has a Schnauzer or a Maltese as a house pet, and they're cute dogs, but I'm partial to bigger dogs. I love the devotion of a Lab, but we had a German shepherd that was so protective of us kids. I'd haf'ta say those are my favorite breeds of dogs, and the combination of them makes a great animal. But, you know, I think I can state as a fact that our German shepherd saved my life or at least kept me from being bunged up worse than I was."

"Oh, yeah? What happened?" Leah asked.

"It was about thirteen or fourteen years ago. I think I was about nine or ten. This one evening one of the cows had not made her way up to the barn when it was time for milking. At that time we herded the milk cows into a fenced field where they could graze during the days. Anyway, this big Guernsey was about ready to calve so I went out to look for it. There was a row of hedge trees that lined the far fence of the pasture. I thought if she'd calved, that's where she might be. Let it be said that I seldom went anywhere outdoors without Chief being with me. Just as I figured, under the hedge trees, there stood Daisy with her new calf. This wasn't her first calf, and if I'd been more on the ball, I would've remembered that she wasn't the epitome of gentle bovine when she was a new momma. The calf was really new, but though she was still a bit wobbly, she was standing alright and had even begun to nurse. Daisy had backed away from her as I started to walk closer to them. Smart me! I was concentrating on checking out the calf, and I just wasn't paying attention to Mom. Anyway, all of a sudden I realized that the freight train I was hearing was that big old cow barreling down on me, and before I realized what was going on, I had been tossed around a little and thrown face down into a rut in the pasture. I remember looking up to see she had stepped back and was going to charge me again. Thank goodness, Chief decided he better step in." Logan snapped his fingers and said, "Just like that, he dashed between me and her, barking up a storm and nipping at her legs. I was able to get up then and scramble over the fence beyond the hedge row."

Leah was watching Logan closely in the moonlight. "Ouch! Were you hurt?"

"She bummed up my ribs on one side, but I was okay. Had a few good bruises though for a couple of days. But you know? I don't know what the outcome of that little scuffle would have been without Chief. I do think he might have been a life saver that day."

Leah felt her own ears getting colder, and she knew Logan, with only his red and gold sweater, was probably even colder. "Let's go back to the car. If I'm getting chilled, you've got'ta be freezing."

As they returned to the car, Leah put her arm into the crook of his. "You're right. The fresh air did me a lot of good. I feel better, and I hope you do, too. Thank you for this."

The warm air from the car's heater felt good, and the ride home was of a less somber mood. Logan parked the car in the driveway and walked Leah to the door. "We had a sad evening, but, Leah, I did have a very nice evening. I'll be here another week, and I know you have to go back to school soon so would you like to get a pizza this Wednesday? Seems the least I can do since I cheated you out of one tonight."

"That would be great. I'd like that, too." Leah hesitated. *"Awkward. Surely he sees 'Awkward" sprawled out in bid ol' letters across my forehead. I mean in big, bright red letters across my forehead."* She squeezed his hand that she had grabbed and turned and ran up the steps to the deck. Whispering, she turned around and said, "Good night, Logan. I had a wonderful time."

Chapter Six

"To See That I Care"

Leah laughed at the inconsistencies of her mind. Sunday afternoon she had been thinking Christmas break was quite long enough, and she had been mentally inviting an early trip back to school. Maybe to clean the small space of her dorm room. Maybe to make a head start on some of the required reading for the next history session. Maybe to even skim the first chapter of her dreaded econ text. Certainly nothing exciting, but, on the other hand, she hadn't anticipated anything exciting in Glendale. That was her mental state before Sunday evening with Logan.

Now it was late Wednesday afternoon, and she was eagerly anticipating the evening with a young Marine home on leave. She remembered the tenderness he had shown when the little dog had been struck. It had been a bit of a contradiction in her expectations of the young warrior. She replayed the memory of the walk along the bluffs above the Chariton River and the quiet conversation which had come so easily. Was he always that comfortable to be with?

"Why do you care? He's a nice way to spend an evening." Leah made a face at the image in the mirror.

"Wouldn't matter if he could talk or not. After tonight, you'll probably be bored, anyway. Or maybe he'll be bored. No diff."

She pulled her blonde hair away from her face, swirled it around her finger and thumb at the back of her head and clamped the hair with an ebony barrette. Several small strands fluttered away from the clasp, but that was all part of the effect. Before stabilizing her hair, she had donned a white turtle neck sweater. Now she added a plaid, flannel long sleeved shirt. Paul would have said it hinted of "rugged". For a pizza date on a Wednesday evening, she figured that shirt with Lee Riders would be appropriate and she would not appear "eager."

Logan had called earlier in the afternoon. "I'll pick you up around seven, and we can grab a sandwich or pizza. Then we can see what's going on in our fair city."

A few minutes before that hour, the doorbell rang. Leah's dad ushered in Logan and invited him to sit. "She can't be too much longer. I heard the hair dryer a few minutes ago. That's usually a sign the finishing touches are being completed. What is it they say? A woman's hair is her crown?"

Logan commented, "That's probably rightly so. In my family, the women are the only ones who get to wear such a head piece. Any crown any of our men would ever have would be covered by a ball cap, anyway. I haven't started wearing one yet because I figure my time will come soon enough. Baldness runs in my family on Mom's side, and I've been informed that the gene is passed down from that parent. Furthermore, they say wearing a cap sometimes inhibits the circulation. Fact or fiction...I'm not taking any chances. If I become bald, then I'll have to wear a cap. Either that or have my dome scorched."

Ted Weeks seemed to enjoy talking with another young man besides his own sons.

"Leah was telling me of the little dog that was run over Sunday night. That was unfortunate." He paused, and then added. "It was probably a pet that had run away from someone there in those apartments. What did you do with it?"

Logan spoke softly. "We have a little area under a row of trees about 50 or 60 feet from the barn. It's a spot where we've buried pets before that have died. In fact, I don't even remember the first pet we buried there." He was quiet briefly, and then continued. "I suppose the first pet we buried probably was a calf whose mom had refused it and we had taken it in to bottle feed. It didn't live too long, as I recall, but I know that I and my sis got pretty attached to it. I guess animals kind of know when something's wrong with a new born, and some mothers will just reject their own babies. I don't even remember what was wrong with it. In fact, I was so small maybe I never did know. Anyway, we have a couple of dogs and a couple of cats buried there, although the cats just usually disappear. Barn cats mostly. I had to make a pretty shallow grave at that on Monday morning with the ground being as frozen as it is, but I covered it over with some big rocks."

As Leah quietly entered the living room, she saw her dad listening to Logan with interest. Mr. Weeks was a large man, and as he stood between the living room and the dining room, he almost filled the archway. Hearing Leah come into the room, he turned his gaze to her and smiled. "Have a good time, but let your mom know you're leaving."

Leah walked past her dad and into the kitchen. *"Occurs to me he could've just as easily conveyed that bit of news to Mom as I could. Maybe even easier, but I suppose it gives him an extra minute to size up Logan. Hmmmm, guess that's okay. I guess dads just do that sort of thing."*

Leah seated herself in the leather seat of Logan's dad's car and waited as Logan walked around to the driver's side of the car. No need to unlock the car doors since in their small town no one locked their car doors. Ever.

As they drove away from the house, he looked at her again, this time acknowledging her person. He appreciated the petite figure beside him.

"Which pizza place for you? We have Ziggy's Pizza, the Pit Stop, or Italian Village. And then, too, we have Ziggy's Pizza, there's the Pit Stop, or the Italian Village. Aaaannndd, we have AJ's. The list is way long. I guess you'll have to choose from that assortment. Too mind boggling for me."

Leah grinned. "Well, since we were headed to the Pit Stop Sunday evening, why don't we try that again? Besides, they have fresh salads. Then I won't eat as much pizza." Then to herself, "*I think I'd even eat a peanut butter and jelly because I really enjoy being with him. Now I wish I hadn't worn this dumb, plaid shirt. Should've gone with something a little dressier, not quite so much the lumberjack look. Too late now.*"

In the Pit Stop Logan chose a booth toward the back of the room and away from the drafty, front door. The establishment was an older building but had been a restaurant of some kind for all the years Leah remembered. There was a time when pool tables had been in the back, and there had been a time when it specialized in large, corn fed, gristle-free, grilled steaks. Now the Pit Stop created thin crust pizzas with mountain high cheese and with sauce not too sweet. And all this on carpet that had been shampooed, then shampooed, and finally shampooed again. Food inspectors sporadically surveyed the faded, colorless carpet and begrudgingly gave pass marks. Music that played from the time the ovens were heated to the last minutes the doors closed at night featured the vocals of George Strait, Willie Nelson, and any voice with a western or country twang.

Leah sat with her back to the door as Logan seated himself across the table. A tall high school junior took their order of pizza and salads and brought their requested drinks, a beer for Logan and a Coke for Leah.

"When do you go back to school?" Logan asked. "On Sunday? I'll be leaving this Friday morning." He had picked up the Mozzarella cheese shaker and rolled it back and forth between his palms. "I really did enjoy Sunday night…well, except for the little dog incident." Shifting his attention, he said, "I still can't believe I didn't see you in high school."

She watched his hands as he rolled the shaker. Fingernails were clean and trimmed. Thank you. Dirty fingernails were a real take-away. "Well, there was one afternoon you noticed me in high school."

Logan looked puzzled.

"Sheesh, I do leave a mark in men's memories, don't I? Do you remember one Sunday afternoon at AJ's when you tackled a guy who had no business even being there? Let alone being a total jerk? He was just obnoxious. As it were, I'm the one who caught a tap to my jaw. Come to think of it, a picture of that swollen jaw made it to the pages of our year book. Yessirree! I really leave 'em wanting more." Leah was trying to muster a pretentious pout on her lips but failed, and the grimace turned into a grin.

"No way! Of course I remember that day. And I do, too, remember you." Logan's eyes were wide as he leaned across the table. "I had wanted to see about taking you home, but you were surrounded by all your little Florence Nightingales. In fact, I think Sarah was right in the middle of that circle, and I was supposed to be big brother taking care of little sister. Dang, I just can't believe I'd forgotten that was you. Shows you how tuned in I was, doesn't it?"

Leah was pleased that he did remember and that he had brought forth feelings of concern over her.

"Do you know what ever happened to the kid that was kicked in the stomach?" Logan leaned back in the booth again. "He was pretty fast in football, and as I recall, he was a freshman or sophomore when I was a senior."

"That was Ryan James. He still came over here some weekends, but that whole car load of guys eventually went back to dating girls from their own school. Or most of them did. Ryan was in my class, and after graduation I think he went on to the University of Arizona on a baseball scholarship. I think one or two of those guys who came out of Arizona went into the pros, but I'm pretty sure Ryan wasn't one of them."

Leah watched Logan's hands which were no longer fiddling with the cheese shaker but were folded casually in front of him on the table. She wondered how often they were idle. "Ryan was a nice guy and had called me some before that afternoon. I think he even called a couple of times after that. We remained friends, but he just slipped out of my life."

The conversation continued with recollections of sports between Glendale and Mission Falls and of the individuals on those teams. The salads, which served as a tasty prelude to the pizza, were enjoyed. When the pizza arrived, Leah took a great deal of time eating two slices. Cheese and Italian sausage were to be appreciated, but even more valuable was the time she was spending with Logan. As it was an evening mid-week, no customers waited for their booth so they felt no need to be rushed. Eventually, every morsel of food in front of them had been devoured, and there was no excuse to linger.

Logan paid the bill at the cash register in the front of the dining room while Leah buttoned her coat and prepared to leave. As she picked up her small clutch purse and turned from the booth, she bumped into a young man.

"Whoa," came a friendly voice. "Leah Weeks. Must I always be a buffer to you? But it's a nice job to have if you can get it."

She took a moment to look at the smiling face of the tall, young man from Mission Falls.

"Oh, my gosh! Ryan James! What a surprise! How nice to bump into you, and I mean that literally. I don't think I've seen you since high school." She put her finger to her chin and said, "Let me see. You're maybe just a skooch taller, but otherwise you look the same." She was looking up into the same dark lashed eyes she remembered from four years ago. "A lot of students go away and gain their 20 freshman pounds, but you didn't, or if you did, you shook them off. You look great."

Ryan replied, "You look pretty fine yourself. You haven't changed much, either. Even the hair's about the same. Did I hear you were going to U of I?"

"I have this semester to finish, and then I'll be done," she replied. "I was really lucky because I was able to schedule all my classes in four years. At Iowa you're doing good if you're not there an extra semester. Then I get to start job hunting. I'll be putting some resumes together this next month. How about you?" As she continued to catch up, she sensed Logan's presence beside her. "Logan, do you remember Ryan James? He's from Mission Falls, and I haven't seen him since high school. Ryan, this is Logan Cummings. You probably played baseball against each other. Football, too."

"How ironic! What little life passages are being played out here right now?" she mused. She assumed Logan made the connection to the earlier conversation that

had passed between them. As Logan and Ryan reminisced with memories of ball games, Leah was given time to study Ryan. Indeed, he hadn't changed much. He had always been tall but *"Give me a break,"* she thought. *"How do I know tall? To me, everyone's tall."* But he had not gained weight, and, in fact, was handsome in his Arizona University colors. She wondered if he remembered Logan as the other contender in the confrontation from several years ago.

As Leah studied him, they were joined by a very pretty lady about her own age. She stood beside Ryan and put her arm through his. Logan turned and offered to him, "We're just leaving this booth, so why don't you and your date take it?"

"Ryan, it was good to see you again," Leah said. And including his date in her remarks, she added, "Enjoy the pizza." No further introductions were offered.

As they walked to the car, Leah noted, "Now how timely was that?"

Logan grinned and replied, "Yeah, stars are lining up in our universe tonight." She hesitated as Logan opened the passenger's door. This little country girl was learning dating etiquette, but it still made her uncomfortable. It was her hope the date wasn't over just because they'd eaten pizza. She wanted the night to continue.

Logan backed from the parking spot and said, "How about driving along Chariton River upstream? Dad said that after the big freeze two weeks ago, some of the ice on the river started breaking up, refroze, and now there's some huge ice jams north of Center City. Or do you have to get back for anything?"

If Logan could have heard a carbon of her emotional self, he would have heard a resounding, *"Yes!!!"* Demurely she replied. "Cool. I'd like to see that, too. But do you think we'll be able to see much in the night?"

"I guess we'll find out."

Leah leaned forward, resisting the grasp of the seat belt, and asked, "Mind if I get a country station?"

Logan laughed. "The dial is yours. Dad usually listens to public radio or a talk station. Let's hear some music. Country, please."

The radio had a search button, and she found a station featuring the voice of Alan Jackson. "Ahhhh, good," she critiqued.

The drive found the huge ice jam. They could see the mountain of ice from the road. Logan turned the car around in the middle of the deserted, gravel road and with the nose of the car pointed towards the river, flicked the headlights to high beam.

"Wow, that's mammoth. If the ice melts quickly, everything down stream will be flooded, won't it? And yet, if it takes its time melting, and this doesn't move from here, there'll be flooding upstream, too, won't there? Anything they can do about it?" she asked.

"I'm not sure. I think there's a means of dynamiting some of it loose, but the weather has to be just right. I suppose that would be a job for the DNR."

Logan pulled the car to the side of the road, maneuvering it to a place where Leah could open the door without being blocked by snow which had been bladed into piles along the side of the road. They scrambled over the snow, Leah mentally thankful she had worn her lace up, rubber soled boots. The river ran about 30 yards from the path of the road, a road which had been constructed years earlier and that ran only slightly elevated from the banks of the river. Because the road was nearly level then with the river itself, annual spring thaws caused the river to overflow its banks and flood the road and surrounding farm land. It didn't take county supervisors long to demand state and federal funds to redirect the road along another course or else to elevate the road. Monies had been directed to rebuild the road further from the river and on a higher level, and at the same time had provided levee control over some of the flooding.

Logan grabbed Leah's hand as they walked down the slope to the river. At the river's edge, she noted he could have dismissed the hold and was glad he didn't. The moon which was nearing a full stage the previous Sunday evening was now bright with reflected light. The river was running quietly so as not to disturb the young people's mood. About six feet from the river bank they found a fallen tree limb from a previous flood. It had been blown free of snow so Leah sat on it. Logan stood a moment looking at the ice jam and then joined her.

"It's such a small river," he began, "but even its miniscule being can create such a large jam." He paused. "Do you ever wonder what the effect of one person might have if he ever really sat down and put his mind to it? This is just a small river in little old Iowa. I think the world looks at our little state as though we're pretty insignificant. Like we're the root of what? Technology? Scientific thinking? Arts? Can't think of much." Logan continued to gaze at the icy river and the ice jam. "Then I think of what small part of all this I am. I'm talking pin-head significance. And yet I'm told that I'm important.

Logan took his gaze from the ice flow and looked at her. She saw his face relax and watched the smile broaden his lips. "Well, here's another observation, I'll make. I think ice jams make me philosophical. Or then again, maybe being around you makes me feel important."

Leah smiled. "Let's go with the ice jam."

The night air was cold, but she was impervious to its bite. And even if she were freezing, she did not want to break this mood. They continued to absorb the magic of the full moon and the drama of the ice jam, but eventually they agreed they should go back to the car. The frosty log had steadfastly refused to show any hospitality or provide any warmth to their backsides.

"Come on, let me give you a hand up the hill," Logan invited.

Leah welcomed the gloved hand, not because she needed the assistance, but because she welcomed the gesture itself.

Logan took a slow measured time returning to Glendale, and after the car found the city limits, it continued its leisurely drive up and down the town's side streets.

At one point Leah said, "This is where I went to grade school. My kindergarten teacher was here with the dinosaurs. I'm sure she had pictures of them. I was scared to death of her, and I hated school."

Logan laughed. "I went to Lincoln Elementary on the south side of town. Rode the school bus in from the farm and thought I was one of the big boys when the guys two years older than me let me sit with them. One of the bus drivers was a young college student who drove our bus before he had classes in the mornings at the community college. He and his girlfriend would drive by our house on Sunday evening, and they would throw pennies and nickels and dimes where he stopped the bus near the driveway. Then, when Sarah was standing there in the midst of those coins on Monday morning, and keep in mind this was when she was in kindergarten, he would open the doors of the bus and point out all those coins around her. He told her the angels must have thrown them out, and she was to be a good girl in school because they would be watching."

Leah laughed aloud. "That was our Sarah? When did she catch on?"

Logan laughed and said, "For all I know she still believes it."

The evening eventually drew to an end, and Logan walked her to her door. "I can't believe how much I've enjoyed Sunday night and tonight. I wish I'd found you when I first came home on leave. The last four days have flown. I mean they've flown." He stopped and looked at her. "Now I'm wanting to see you again, and I have to leave Friday morning for Pendleton."

Leah leaned against the stair railing to the deck that was the threshold to the back door. Her voice was low, and she heard it as a whisper. "I've loved the time, too, and I have to go back to school on Sunday."

"May I write to you?" Logan was asking. "Or better yet, call? At least when I get a chance. And I'll let you know where I'll be stationed. I hope you'll let me hear from you."

"Oh, you can count on it." As she looked up, the full moon exposed to her a face of gentleness, mixed with questions. Then he slipped both arms around her and pulled her closer to him. Leah's face was at the small of his neck, and she smelled the smoky scent of Stetson. She raised her face, and he gently kissed her lips. The mouth was soft, and the kiss was slow. Her arms encircled his shoulders and neck.

Leah hadn't dated much, but other good night kisses had not brought feelings such as this. She had dreaded for the evening to be over, and she hated for this embrace and kiss to end.

She leaned into his chest. The leather jacket was cool in the night, but she cherished its feel on her cheek. He had not loosened his embrace. She tilted her head back, and he kissed her again.

"I could do this for a very long time, and please be informed that I'm pretty much of a novice." As he kissed her again, she added, "But I think you're a great teacher. Wish we had time for more lessons."

Logan grinned and hugged her tighter. He whispered before he kissed her again, "Let's make an appointment to do this the very next chance we get. My next leave."

Finally, he released his embrace and stepped away. "I'll call you tomorrow. You can give me your address at I of U then with your phone number."

He turned to leave, and then turned back. He put his arms around her again. This time he very gently kissed the corners of her eyes.

She was startled and looked at him in surprise.

"That's to make sure you can SEE how much I already care for you." He laughed at her surprise, then turned and strode to his car.

Leah watched as he settled into the front seat. She touched the corners of her eyes, turned, and walked into the house.

Chapter Seven

Making a Home

Four years away from home at a university had given Leah time to stretch the tendons of family ties. The first semester of university life demanded that she return home to Glendale almost every weekend. She excused those visits by telling friends that her folks were having a difficult time letting go of their little girl, but she didn't admit aloud that she needed those trips as well. Into the second semester, though, she started the process of becoming a full time university student and made the trip home at spring break only. Sophomore year brought a clean separation. As of the second fall she hadn't missed the family or home though her parents still made trips to school once a month to see her.

Leah graduated from the university that spring. With a degree in business, she had taken the big step away from rural Iowa and had moved to Des Moines. Her Hill Crest dormitory roommate who had grown up in the state's capital had encouraged her to "live a little" and experience life in a metropolitan area, and Des Moines was as close to metropolitan as that small-town Iowa girl had lived. Both young ladies shared an apartment in a western suburb, and Leah fit quite easily into a life underwriter's position in one of the larger insurance companies.

The Des Moines area provided weekend activity that kept both ladies busy. The downtown arena was a scene of art festivals, farmers' markets, and a plethora of music venues. Warm weather provided opportunities to walk or bike around lakes, through parks, or along shaded trails. If she had been interested, there was ample opportunity to golf. Winter gave her a chance to see concerts and Broadway performances which had taken to the road.

In all that was introduced to her, both as opportunities and as new friendships, Leah did not dismiss Logan's presence from her mind. She dated a young man from her workplace, and although she had been informed he was 'a catch' and was on his way up the ladder, she hadn't felt a connection to move on with the relationship. Other dates were made with other young men, but none interested her as much as the phone calls and letters from the young man from Glendale.

After graduation from ISU, and with the economy unsettled, Logan had decided that would be a good time to try the service. Others might have chosen the Marines before they went to college, but he had been fortunate to earn a partial football scholarship at Ames and had elected to play ball. So, while Leah was pursuing a career in Des Moines, Logan was fulfilling his commitment to the Marines. From time to time worries of war had passed through the minds of those in power, but Logan's promise to the Marines expired before the Gulf War became a reality.

From the time he had entered high school Logan had assumed he would work with his dad running their seven hundred plus acre farm. That was just the understanding. He had graduated with a degree in agronomy in 1984, a time when farmers were struggling with high interest rates and low market prices. Logan's dad had not made investments in more machinery and wasn't buying land, though more land was available as neighbors were falling into bankruptcy.

The military had been valuable experience for Logan. Just as Leah had left the small world of her rural community and had been introduced to new sights and sounds, he, too, had seen and experienced events he otherwise wouldn't have. Opportunity had allowed him to visit three continents and tour the Pacific.

After three years in Des Moines, Leah's roommate Chris had met a young man who worked as a UPS delivery man by day and played in a local blues band by night. The two moved in together, leaving an apartment and sole rent to Leah. As for Leah, when Logan was home on leave, she valued the time being with him and missed him when he was gone. At the end of those same three years it had become evident to Leah she had lived enough of her life in Des Moines.

Logan's four years with the military ended within months of Chris's abandonment of Leah and their shared apartment. His phone calls and letters told her he would be home in April. When he arrived, Logan spent every weekend in West Des Moines.

At the end of May the lease to the apartment expired.

At the end of May Logan asked Leah to leave Des Moines and move home.

At the end of May they became engaged.

*   *   *   *   *   *

The transition to life in southern Iowa proceeded exceedingly well. Leah returned to her parents' home and to her old room in the upstairs of the two story house. Her mom actively became the unofficial wedding planner. This was her only daughter and, fortunately, Leah approved of most of her mother's ideas. A position as office manager in the doctors' clinic was brought to her attention, and with her degree in business and her experience as a life underwriter, she was a perfect fit. It didn't hurt at all, either, that one of the doctors had been the family doctor since the clinic had opened.

Logan had stepped into the role of the farm manager with equal ease. Although the elder Mr. Cummings was considering retiring, he wasn't quite ready to hand over those reins even to his son. Logan found a small, brick house less than a mile from the clinic, and that became their home until the time his dad decided he didn't want to farm anymore.

When a farmer reaches an age that's designated as his time of retirement, the decision to retire doesn't always coincide with his chronological age. To arise every morning and not have a purpose for that day can be deflating, even devastating, plunging many a farmer into deep depression. Most farmers have found that happiness is achieved in doing work that is "the taking from and giving back to the soil"… the core that brings them pleasure and gives them a sense of accomplishment. Retirement can be that elusive, frightening time in which they no longer feel that daily sense of achievement nor look forward to the day with anticipation. Does there come an age when there are no longer goals? No longer aspirations? Is that the final dismissal of youth?

The red brick house was small but served as a cozy home in which love abided for the newlyweds. In time, retirement did come for the senior Mr. and Mrs. Cummings. When the older couple moved into a smaller house in town, the younger couple moved into Logan's boyhood home. They made improvements in the house: new kitchen cupboards, and a new half bath off the kitchen, always depending upon cattle and grain prices.

Leah had always lived in the town of Glendale. The farm life was new, but she loved the big frame house. She particularly loved the animals, except she soon learned that to make attachments to the cattle and their new calves was a mistake, a heartbreaking mistake. Calves were born and 'fed out' for one primary purpose and that was to sell at market. Noooooo, not to get acquainted with nor attached to the cute little black faced Angus calves. They just grew up, and she learned she couldn't bear to watch the semi-stock trucks arrive and load her pets to auction or market. In fact, she learned not to be around at all on the days the truck was scheduled to make its pick up.

*   *   *   *   *   *   *

At the first hints of spring, farmers' activities shift from neutral directly into high gear. Logan watched from the kitchen window as warmer days brought melting snow and disappearing ice, and the cold ground became soft and muddy. He usually sold off much of his livestock before winter ushered in sleet and snow; thus he left himself with only breeding stock. Calves born in the spring each year were fed out and then sold at auction in the fall, leaving him with just a few chores in the winter. When he wasn't checking and repairing machinery, he often spent mornings in Glendale at the co-op catching up on local news, discussing market prices, and throwing in a few views regarding the politicians in DC and their seemingly disdain for the plight of the struggling Midwestern farmer.

Spring with its budding trees and greening pastures stirred an excitement within him. Now standing and looking across the yard at the barn and the feed lot, he was eager to start readying the fields for corn planting. He usually alternated crops of soy beans and corn, and this spring he would be planting corn. Whatever crop he chose to raise, he told himself, was the crop that would become the most expensive to plant and would usually be the crop that brought the lowest prices in the fall.

Leah watched her husband as he poured himself another mug of strong coffee and leaned against the kitchen counter. In the five years since they had moved into his parents' homestead, she had watched as he stepped into the role for which he had prepared. He still wore Levi boot cut jeans, and the brown, leather belt had been loosened one notch. With increased spring activities, the belt would be tightened back to the third hole again. The hands were strong and calloused, and the arms and chest were muscular and hard. She smiled as she stood at the door of the dining room and remembered his foreboding that he would lose his hair, just as the other men in his family did. He wasn't bald, but they both had remarked as the hair at the sides of his forehead was receding. He was still handsome, and she made sure he knew that. Most of all, she loved his eyes. She decided brown eyes denoted strength. Therefore, the kindness she saw there might have been a surprise to some. They might have misconstrued that trait as weakness. Never!

She walked across the kitchen and handed his faded denim jacket to him. "I could use some air. Let's use this day when the trees aren't swaying. We can walk down to the pond, and maybe it'll ward off another episode of cabin fever for you."

Logan took another swig of coffee from the mug, and then poured the remainder down the drain.

"Sounds like a plan, and at the same time, I'll show you just where I'll be putting your gazebo. I think when Mom and Dad come out, Mom will get some enjoyment in sitting in it. Hell, Dad will too." Snapping his jacket, he opened the kitchen door, and then stepped aside for her to pass.

"Still the gentleman," she noted to herself. The early April sunshine was deceiving, but not unpleasant. She flipped up the hood of the Glendale football jacket to protect her ears from the surprising breeze and pushed her hands into the pockets. Logan shortened his normal pace so she could match his stride, and they walked down the slope to the pond. Strolling along the edge of the small body of water, Logan noted he would restock the pond with more fish as the days warmed. With the addition of new fish to be caught, he would make more time to spend with his dad.

As they followed the path, Logan spied a flat, round rock about the diameter of a golf ball. He stepped in front of her and deliberately kicked it down the trail. Leah walked quickly to the rock and kicked it further. Logan took a turn, kicking it much further, but still on the trail. The childish game continued as they made their way back to the house.

Both of Leah's hands were out of her pockets as she walked to the rock. She said, "Guess I'll have to show you how to do this."

Her kick put the rock still on the path but in line for a small sapling at its edge. Logan approached the rock and looking over his shoulder at Leah, said, "Ha! Watch it hit the tree. I be the champ." With his boast, he kicked but cast the stone at least two feet beyond the young oak.

Leah ran to the rock, and taunting her good-natured husband, kicked the rock and watched as it hit the tree. She laughed and shouted boisterously, 'No, I be the champ. Me thinks you be the chump." She jumped up and down, pumping her arms in the air.

Logan grinned a big grin, then grabbed her at the waist and fell to the ground, rolling with her on top of him. He rolled her over into the remnants of a snow mound and straddled her. She was laughing as he pinned both arms above her head. Then holding both wrists with one hand, he tickled her. Very slowly he moved his fingers under her arm and along her rib cage and under her jacket.

Leah kicked and laughed until her laughter turned to pleas. "No," she screamed. Logan's fingers stopped their gentle prodding, but he remained lightly on top of her. "Not before we determine who's the champ around here. Now who would that be?" He looked up into the sky as if listening for an answer. Soon he heard a soft affirmation.

"You would be the champ. There would NEVER be a doubt. Now let me up, or you're going to be so sorry. And maybe wet."

He grinned, then leaned down over her face. "I just wanted to make sure you knew." And with that he released her wrists and kissed her gently on her lips. She wrapped her arms around his neck and responded to his kiss.

"Now help me up. Let me get to the bathroom." She started running up the path to the house, but turning back over her shoulder, she yelled. "Oh, you are soooo wrong. You still be the chump. I be the champ."

Chapter Eight

A Promise Made

The lights in the doctors' waiting room were turned off as the last patient had exited the clinic. From her desk Leah saw the hallway was bare. The wooden pockets, now empty of any patients' charts, clung to the walls beside the doors to the exam rooms. The building's interior had been painted as recently as a year ago, but the mushroom colored walls already were smudged with dirt and oil of worried patients' hands. She smiled as she noted the majority of the marks were closer to the floor and hinted at the shorter heights of small children. How many reluctant boys and girls had trailed their nervous fingers along the plaster? The neutral color had been chosen exactly for that reason, to camouflage those marks. Even realizing the practicality of that color selection, she had noted to herself at the time that the color made the trip to the exam rooms even more depressing. If she had been asked, she would have chosen a bright fun color, such as a paprika, pumpkin, or even a lime green, but as the office manager, she hadn't been consulted. One of the doctor's wives had made that choice.

The pictures on the walls did speak of the medical personality of the building, and their choice had found favor with her. The selections were made by the doctors themselves; at least that's what the staff had been led to believe. Leah knew that of the three doctors who formed the clinic, Dr. Charles Green had the most dominant personality. And behind his personality was the even stronger drive of his much younger wife. Leah knew if the doctor's spouse had preferred modern art or less traditional art, and it was rather surprising that she didn't, that preference would be displayed on the walls of the corridor. As it were, children and their moms could study the works of Norman Rockwell if they so desired, but as far as she knew, no one had actually studied any of the pictures, and probably very few had even noticed. The mother whose child was screaming from the pain of an ear infection was not in a mood for art, nor was the child who had just caught his fingers in the clutches of a car door. Leah had come to the conclusion when the art work had been hung, that the doctors and the staff would comprise the majority of the observers.

The big, round, generic clock on the wall in the corridor displayed 5:25, as did the more personal clock on her credenza. She was finishing the withholding of taxes from the last of the payrolls and was eager to go home. Logan had called that afternoon as he had made his weekly jaunt into the co-op. Friday nights were her favorite evenings. Although Saturday was the end of his work week, Friday was the end of hers. Sometimes they would attend a high school sports event, especially during the fall's football season and at least the home games, and sometimes they would check out a movie in town. But her favorite evenings, the ones she looked forward to most, were those evenings they spent at home together. She knew the routine, and that made her smile.

In the afternoon Logan would call her office and ask what she wanted for dinner, or, in the typical Iowa jargon, would ask, "What do you want for supper?" It would never surprise him when she responded, "I want pizza from the Pit Stop."

Then the routine would be "Pizza again? Don't you want something different? How about chicken or a fish night? Or even Bar-B-Q?"

She would usually reply, "That sounds good, too. This is fast food night, and I'm not cooking, so let's get what you want." Then when she walked through the door into the kitchen, invariably she would smell the aroma of pizza from the Pit Stop. Fortunately, they both liked pizza and even the same kind of pizza, full of pepperoni, mushrooms, and loaded with gooey cheese. On those nights that they went to a ball game or to a movie, they might be satisfied with a quick hamburger at AJ's or Kentucky Fried Chicken. It was just fun to play their little game, even when they both knew what would be the edible outcome.

Leah tidied the unfinished paper work and logged off her computer. She rolled up the Roman shade of the west window so that the Swedish Ivy on the credenza would receive light over the week-end. Then from behind the door she pulled down the red, wool jacket with the big, black buttons and slid it over her arms. Much of the south wall opposite the door was covered with a large mirror which served the single purpose of making her office appear larger. As she buttoned her jacket, Leah studied the image in the mirror. From time to time she was startled to see how her appearance was changing.

The blonde hair she had taken for granted in her youth was not gray, but was a much more subtle hue. She had detected just a few gray hairs and had just recently begun using an ash blond tint. No one had commented on any difference so she hoped no one had detected the cover-up. She didn't think of herself as vain, but she wasn't appreciating changes that were occurring that brought attention to the fact that she was aging. *"Let's say maturing,"* she thought. The long hair from her younger years was short now and styled with a slight wave that was loose and was arranged in an unfettered fashion. She got by with a quick blow dry by running her fingers through applied foam while standing on her head. Well, almost.

Somewhere it was dictated that blondes were to have a very light pink complexion, but in Leah's case, the summer often brought a tan. As the season left, so did the brown pigmentation, and eventually as the summer sun faded into fall, she reverted to her spring and fair complexion. She was grateful that she did tan because she knew some of her blonde friends in school had not carried on a loving relationship with the sun, and, in fact, had often avoided it. But the image in the mirror now showed only a few traces of the sun from last summer.

She wore little make-up and wasn't interested in learning about it. She did edge sable mascara along her eyelids and darkened her eye brows slightly. Her brown eyes had not lost their intensity and were quite animated when she was excited about something.

Leah turned sideways and reviewed her reflection full length. At thirty nine she spied just the beginning of the effects of gravity. Others may not notice, but she was quite aware. She knew she would not maintain her high school weight of one hundred sixteen pounds so she wasn't too dismayed that she had kept her gain at nine pounds. She was physically active in spite of her desk job's responsibility. "I *mean being the wife of a farmer…there is no way you're going to be a couch princess,"* she mused.

She gave the bottom of her jacket a tug as it had bunched slightly over the quilted vest she had worn and pulled her black leather purse from the bottom drawer of her desk. She needn't lock up tonight since the maintenance crew would be there until after ten or eleven.

Driving home was always a pleasant respite of the day except in the winter when roads were icy. Driving to the sanctuary of her farm home gave her a chance to wind down. She had once said to Logan, "Seeing Glendale in my rear view mirror is the best part of my day." Not so much that she was eager to leave her work day but more that she was eager to be home with Logan again.

The radio was usually tuned to a country station, but sometimes she listened to her own CDS which ranged from some new age, some old music from the 80's, or even a few classic oldies from her folks' era. This evening she dismissed work and anticipated a quiet evening with Logan.

Leah drove through the main street of Glendale. Maneuvering through the small town was not an elaborate exercise in driving skills. In fact, if a driver's license were based upon skills required to drive in Glendale, a person could probably qualify by reading a <u>Learning to Drive for Dummies Manual</u>, if such a book were written. That being said, there was still some expertise in driving required if you were between the ages of sixteen and twenty-five. Young men would be graded on their ability to shift gears at a respectable number of RPMs and on the amount of base applied to their car's audio system. Young ladies felt merely the need to conquer steering and applying make-up while giving at least some scant attention to the tail lights of the car ahead.

Moving through Glendale on the main street was slowed by less than a half dozen stop signs and only three traffic lights. Leah chuckled to herself as she drove home, "It doesn't take long to make an exit even in 'heavy rush hour' traffic."

Leah left town and continued on the north paved road. The changing of the seasons was a necessary increment of Iowa climate. At 5:30 the sun was heavier in the skies. Like the furry animals that hibernated in the cold winter, it appeared this evening the sun had fattened itself and was appearing more cumbersome above the horizon. In a couple of weeks day light savings time would be erased, and the 5:30 sun she was seeing now would emit the same amount of light she would have then at 4:30.

The autumn was a beautiful Technicolor display this year. The maples and the burning bushes, even the reddened poison ivies around the tree trunks, seemed to strut their colors. Two hardwood maples along her route home always seemed each year to outdo themselves. Each year she watched for the colors of the two trees that grew along a fence as the road began an incline. She observed that God must have poured a bright crimson paint over the tops of them one night each fall and then stood back and watched as the red paint trailed down through the branches in the following days. They were her favorite trees on the route home.

The paved road gave a driver a choice of continuing north or turning west onto gravel. Leah's destination demanded that she turn west. She decreased her speed partly because the gravel was loose and, even more importantly at this time of year, because the heavy sun was now sitting in the road directly ahead of her. Even with the sun shade pulled down and with her sun glasses on, the glare was blinding.

Leah's eyes strained to find the traveled portions of the road. The county's maintenance crew usually did a good job of leveling the surface, but when loads of fresh rock had been applied, ridges of that gravel would lie in furrows along the shoulders' edges. This gravel was new, and perhaps the county worker had not had enough afternoon sun time to finish spreading it before his work day ended.

Even with the glare of a setting sun, the daylight around her was growing dim. Suddenly Leah caught the quick movement of a deer as it darted from the ditch and towards the road. The deer's movement was so quick, it was on the side of the road and racing across in front of Leah's RAV 4 before she had time to realize a logical course of action. But when a deer jumps in front of a moving car, logic seldom factors into any driving decision.

Leah braked hard and twisted the steering wheel away from the path of the doe. The wheels slid in the loose gravel. The RAV 4, instead of moving into the direction of the turn as was demanded, began to fishtail on the road. Leah had no control. She knew after a quick spin to release the pressure on the brake, but the momentum of the spinning tires threw her small SUV into a deep ditch on the opposite side of the road from which it had been directed.

Leah's panic was a terror. As the auto spun wildly in the road, she could only hang onto the steering wheel. All she could do was stay for the ride. And, fortunately, because of her clasped seat belt, she did stay. The vehicle plunged forward into the deep, steep ravine. As the small Toyota left the road, small trees and brush broke and snapped past her windows. She dropped into an eroded steep gully. Then as the auto hit front first, Leah heard the loud bang of the air bag. Immediately, the interior of the car was filled with an acrid smoke or dust. The bag struck her chest and face, possibly saving her life. At the same time that she heard the explosion of the air bag, Leah heard the windshield breaking. Glass burst into the car, covering the front seat, the floors, and herself. Because of the explosion of the air bag, her face was protected from serious cuts from the flying glass. As it were, her ungloved hands and wrists were cut, but her coat had absorbed much of the glass chards, protecting her further.

The RAV 4 finally settled, having exercised its right to have a mind of its own, and stopped its journey. With her face buried in the air bag, she momentarily remained motionless. She pulled herself from the deflating cushion and brought her head up as much as she could at the 90 degree angle at which she sat. The air in the car was compromised by the debris of the air bag explosion, but fresh air through the broken windows gradually leveled the mixture, making it easier to inhale. She paused, collecting her thoughts. She was aware the radio was still playing. *"How appropriate. Eddie Rabbit singing "Driving My Life Away."* She mused. *"Could have been worse. Could have been, "If Tomorrow Never Comes."* She looked at her rear view mirror which was askew but unbroken. She reached up and straightened it, then fussed at herself. "First things first," she laughed aloud. "Make sure you can see out that back window."

With bleeding hands, Leah pushed the now deflated air bag from her chest but then realized it was providing a large amount of support for her. After a few moments more and still trying to gather her senses, she noticed a foreign smell. She identified it as anti-freeze. *"That's logical,"* she rationalized. *"The radiator's smashed."* Although the motor was no longer running, she felt beneath the air bag, found the key in the ignition, and turned it off. She didn't know about the possibility of a car fire but thought that action might make her a little safer.

Leah made a check of her physical being as well as she could. *"Step one,"* she calculated. Although the seat had jolted forward, she could move her feet and legs. No pain there. She could move her arms, shoulders, and torso. Looking into the righted mirror, she saw her face had only a few cuts, but it was bright red and burning from the powder and impact of the air bag.

"Now...step two. Get out of the car." It was apparent to her that nightfall was settling around her. Leah struggled to unfasten her seatbelt and grabbed the door handle. She pulled up and pushed hard against the door, but the door was crumpled and unforgiving. Its glass was cracked but still intact. Before smashing and trying to climb through the window, she decided to try the passenger's door.

Leah tried to climb over the console in the middle of the seats, the console which housed the automatic gear shift and the holder for her CDs, but even before she completed that hike, she could see in the darkness that that door was crumpled, too. From what she could tell, maybe even worse than the driver's side.

She edged her way through chards of broken glass and was grateful she had worn boots instead of the soft flats which was often her shoe choice. Climbing into the back seat, she moved behind the driver's seat. Because that seat had been thrust forward, she had some room to argue with the door. This time, as she jerked hard on the handle, it moved outward. However, the brush against the side of the car refused to allow her to open the door, still holding her prisoner.

Leah pushed again and again. Finally the door was ajar enough that she could squeeze her small, coated frame through. She climbed out, into and onto the stiff, fall bushes. Then she was upright, standing in the dark. She turned and started climbing up the embankment. When she reached the shoulder of the road, Leah sat down. Into the dark she looked deep into the ravine. The tail lights of the RAV 4 were still shining. Leah's shoulders sagged, and she began to cry. As she sobbed tears of relief, she mentally rode the car again as it spun in the road, as it settled into the gully, as she made her escape from the car's steel clutches. She wasn't angry at the blinding sun nor the loose gravel, nor even the innocent deer. She was grateful she was alright. Looking down at her vehicle and unable to see the extent of its damage, Leah knew the situation could have been worse. Much worse.

With the realization of her good fortune, Leah relaxed, and calm overcame her again. In the trial of ridding herself from her unlikely tomb, she had left her purse in the car. There was no way she was going to slide down and crawl back into that thing again tonight. She just wanted to see Logan. "I just want you to put your arms around me and hold me," she moaned.

She stood and decided she would start walking home on her unbroken, somewhat bloody, but still very healthy legs. In the darkness, the moon was trying to make a half-hearted appearance. It sickly offered some light, though not much. She pulled her gloves from her coat pockets. Gingerly, she tried to pull them over her hurting hands but felt pieces of glass in the backs of her fingers. The small pieces of glass snagged against the wool, knit gloves. Donning the gloves was added pain she didn't need, and she wondered if she would cause the slivers to become more embedded. Eventually, she opted to shove her hands, uncovered and still bleeding, into her coat pockets. She began her walk home. Her walk had not taken her far when the headlights of a pickup approached her from behind. As it neared, it slowed. The pickup, which she recognized and loved, screeched to a stop in the middle of the road.

Logan jumped from the cab and ran to her. "Heaven help us, Leah. What are you doing? What's happened?"

He put both arms around her and held her close to him. They stood embraced on the shoulder of the road. He released her and quietly walked with his arm around her to the front of the truck and into the light of the truck's headlamps. He stood back and stared at her.

"Oh, Honey, what happened?" His face displayed as much concern as the sound of his voice. He was never good at concealing his emotions. When he finally could see her red face, burned from the abrasion of the air bag, he was horrified. "Your face is burning red. And you're hurt. I need to know."

Leah leaned against him and cried again, though softly now. Her tears came because of his pain and his fears. She said, "Let's go back where I began walking, and you can see what once was our beautiful little car. But, don't worry. I'm okay. Trust me, though. This little body is going to be sore tomorrow. And, too, you may be able to get my purse from the front seat."

Logan turned the pickup around in the middle of the road and drove back. They didn't have to drive far since she hadn't been walking that long. Logan could see from the skid and sliding marks in the gravel where she had lost control. He shone the headlights across the top of the ravine. The light allowed them to make out a bit of crushed brush, crumpled small trees and the vehicle balanced on the front of its hood. Logan turned the pickup to a different angle and looked ten to twelve feet beyond where the car had settled.

"Oh, good Lord, Leah," he whispered. "Do you realize how close you came to plunging into the Chariton River? Twelve more feet and you wouldn't have stopped where you did. You would have been at the bottom of the river."

She watched him as he sat behind the steering wheel. She felt numb in hearing what he was saying. But as she looked at him, she saw his face grimace, and she saw tears at the corners of his eyes. "Leah, I couldn't stand that."

She leaned across the console of the pickup and put her hand on his at the steering wheel. "Well, guess what, Mr. Cummings. I don't intend to leave you for a long, long time. Let's say another sixty or seventy years. I recognized a find eighteen years ago, and I'm not going to let it go." She looked into his anguished face and then winked.

"Now let's go home. We can call the insurance company and a wrecker tomorrow morning, but for now, I just want to go home. And have some pizza. And a back rub from my hubby."

That Friday afternoon, Logan had driven into the co-op to glean neighborhood news. Before he started home, he had ordered the pizza and some minutes later had picked it up. He had planned on being at the house before Leah arrived, but conversation, futures, and grain prices had held his interest longer than he judged. He had been shocked to find her walking home in the dark and further alarmed when he learned of the accident.

Before they drove home, Logan found a flashlight in the truck's glove compartment and partially walked, but mostly slid to the RAV 4. He managed to pull the back door open far enough to squeeze through and retrieve her purse from the floor of the front seat by climbing over the console and gear shift.

Now Logan reclined on the brown, leather davenport with an embroidered pillow of Leah's making beneath his head. The television set displayed the ten o'clock news, but his mind continued to play the 'what ifs' of that evening….'what if' Leah had nose-dived into the river, 'what if' she had rolled the SUV, 'what if' she hadn't worn her seat belt. He drifted back to reality to enjoy the moment as Leah massaged his legs. She applied lotion to the front and back of his calves and gently squeezed those tight muscles. He jerked and twisted as she ran her fingers along the bottoms of his feet.

"No fair. You forget I'm ticklish," he yelped.

"You sound like a little girl," she laughed. "Besides, my hands just keep ending up on your feet because they run out of room on those short hairy legs of yours."

He laughed and sat up then and put his arm over the back of the couch.

"Want me to rub your back?" he asked.

Pulling her sweater over her head, she laid her head in his lap, closed her eyes, and said, "Ummmm, you're such a smooth talker. You know how I love that, and besides, I think my shoulders are already tightening up."

He squeezed the back of her neck with his fingers and began to gently rub her shoulders. In spite of his hands being rough and calloused, they felt wonderfully soothing. He deftly unsnapped her bra with one hand so he could massage her whole back.

Leah closed her eyes and felt the stiffness leaving her shoulders and back. She luxuriated in the gentleness of his patterned strokes, more the caress.

Logan's voice was husky as he said, "Leah, do you realize what a close call you had this afternoon? Do you realize how close I came to losing you?"

Leah interrupted her bliss and rolled over on her back to see his face. She wrestled out of her bra, then lay back on his lap.

"I hadn't realized how close I had come to going into the river until we drove back. I was scared at the time, but it really didn't soak in." She paused. "Sometimes when I've thought of horrible things that could happen to me, of horrible ways to die, I've been afraid of drowning. It makes me shudder to think that could have happened. I was feeling I had been so lucky I wasn't hurt just in landing in the ravine." She sat up and put her arms around his neck.

Logan held her bare, sore body close to him. For a few minutes neither spoke, but felt pleasure in being close and comforted by each other. Logan pulled back and looked at her face. Then he kissed both her eye lids. She blinked and looked back at him.

"I know. I remember. That's so I can SEE how much you love me," she whispered.

She leaned her head back and studied his countenance. The forehead was higher than it was in years past. *"Funny,"* she mused. *"I've never paid that much attention before, but he's still so handsome."* The farmer tan was less dark now, and she admired the creases in his sunned face. But the eyes still identified him. She had always thought they were beautiful, but now they were somber as they gazed back. They were no longer the eyes of the lad in college nor the eyes of the young Marine. She was looking into the eyes of a gentle man. He was responsible and caring. She felt safe. "And I will always love you, Logan Cummings. You speak of a life without me, but I can't fathom any kind of life without you."

"Well, Sweetie, I'll always be around to take care of you. And if anything ever happened to me, I'd find a way to take care of you. Promise!" He squeezed her to him again and said, "It's early, but let's go to bed. I can spend a whole night of just appreciating you."

Smiling, she disentangled herself from his arms and stood up. She retrieved her sweater and bra from the floor and walked into the bedroom. Logan turned off the television and lights and followed close behind.

*   *   *   *   *   *   *

Dawn made her appearance on schedule through the east windows of Logan and Leah's bedroom. Only Logan saw her and responded to her summons. He rose and ambled into the farm house's kitchen where he made coffee. He walked back to the bedroom, dressed quietly, then left the room, closing the door behind him. He performed his usual toiletries and left the house. Heading the pickup down the driveway, he drove the 12 miles into Glendale. At the kitchen of the county co-op, he purchased four pastries, two doughnuts for himself and two pecan rolls for Leah which were her favorites.

As he drove west towards the farm, he slowed and looked again at the steep ravine Leah had traveled the night before. By now the sun had made a full appearance in the sky behind him. The night had brought a frost. Logan knew the day would be a good one, one he would be able to start combining his corn. Yesterday had been dry, and the field could probably have been worked then, but the risk was still too great to get a huge, cumbersome machine stuck in the mud. He had seen farmers with combines mired so deep, they had broken the axel. Nope, just wasn't worth the risk.

The RAV 4 sat unceremoniously on its bruised red nose. He would call the wrecking or towing company after eight o'clock when they opened. Driving on over the bridge that spanned the Chariton River, Logan noticed several does drinking at its edge. They would be going to bed now that daylight was here. This was the rutting season so he assumed a buck was nearby, watching his harem. They would sleep through the day and come out to graze or forage through the corn at dusk.

He drove on to the farm. Enjoying the serenity of the early morning, he preferred no radio. He drove with his window down, listening to the quiet of the rural countryside, interrupted only by the chirping of early morning songsters. He debated annually his favorite time of the year, and every season he vacillated that the particular season he was experiencing at that time was the best. But this year for sure he knew. Autumn in Iowa was his favorite. And this morning brought it all home.

The day would be sunshine and dry.

His crops looked good.

Leah was safe and with him.

Chapter Nine

The Accident

That spring Logan worked the soil of the farm and anticipated a respectable crop of beans. His breeding stock bore an ample herd. As is the norm, even under his watchful eye, a few mamas proved themselves to be dumb animals and were the cause of losing some calves. Whether they were animals of less intelligence or mothers who weren't really into a nurturing venue, the results were the same. Of his fifty-some head of breeding stock, he also had kept a few heifers from the previous year's stock. The most problems always seemed to come from the inexperienced heifers as they became mothers for the first time.

Logan was sad and also angry when he found a new mother had lain on her newborn. He didn't allow himself to attach feelings for the new calves, but he also wasn't so dispassionate that he couldn't enjoy the new life around him, and he felt such disbelief when any cow, especially a new mother, would be so oblivious to her new baby. And it wasn't just the new mothers who displayed such lack of concern. The older cows also would step on or lay on their young.

Always there would be one or two new moms who had no maternal instincts and who would turn their backs on their babies. This year Logan had been fortunate enough to put an unwanted babe with a mother whose offspring was stillborn and another with a cow who had rolled over on her new one.

A third calf, whose mother had died birthing it, necessitated being fed manually through means of a bottle. In a short time the bottle was replaced with a bucket, a bucket which had a large, protruding rubber nipple at its bottom. That calf became a pet, and the chore of feeding came to Leah in the evenings. Logan fed the calf by the nursing bucket in the mornings, and Leah took over the responsibility in the evenings when she came home from her work.

Although Mr. and Mrs. Logan Cummings had wanted a family, becoming pregnant and carrying a baby full term was an unrealized dream for Leah. Twice she had become pregnant, and twice she had miscarried. Each time brought not only a deep sorrow to both of them, but to Leah came a feeling of guilt. "What's wrong with me?" was also mixed with "Is there some reason I'm being punished?"

Doctors explained to her that no one was at fault, neither she nor Logan. "Take a break," they suggested. "No need to take steps to prevent a pregnancy, but just take things easy. Don't try so hard."

The young couple decided if Leah wasn't pregnant by next spring, they would investigate sources of adoption.

Leah, who deliberately did NOT want to play mom to any cute, black faced calf, who absolutely did not want to get attached to any bovine animal, found herself loving the four legged orphan. As soon as she walked into the house each evening, she changed from her office clothes into jeans and then shorts later when the weather warmed. As she made the trips to the barn, and then mixed the baby formula, she at first assured herself that she could do this babysitting task and remain disinterested. But all was lost when she named the sweet-faced youngster. And what would she name a hungry little orphan, one who had to be kept from the herd so it wouldn't be mistreated by the other mothers? Why Annie, of course. The name came as a perfunctory thought.

Leah held the bucket through the rails of the corral at the side of the barn and smiled a warm gaze of amusement as she watched the calf bump and nudge the bucket against the slats of the fence. The new calf sucked from the large nipple on the bucket, and when its eyes weren't closed in contentment at its meal, she would look curiously under long lashed lids at Leah. Theirs was a meeting of an unsolicited charge and of a perfect innocent. After only one feeding the innocent one became Leah's foster child.

As the summer passed and Annie grew, she was turned into the feeding lots with the other calves. However, she remained Leah's pet and would race to the fence of the lot when she saw her. She appreciated the strokes on her head and neck to her shoulders, and Leah informed Logan somewhere in that summer that her pet would not be among those cattle which would leave in the fall. Logan wasn't surprised and found that dictum to be inarguable. He accepted it without a fuss.

Leah filled her evenings after work learning about gardening, both flowers and vegetables. She froze green beans and corn, made jellies from strawberries and rhubarb, and salsa and tomato juice from her tomatoes. *This sure isn't what I was planning when I was getting a degree in business,"* she mused to herself. But if she had been given an option to be anywhere else, doing anything else, or being with anyone other than Logan, there wouldn't have been the slightest choice.

Logan got a third cutting from his alfalfa for hay bales for his breeding herd's winter feeding and thought there would be enough without having to buy more. More acres this year had been planted in beans, and the fall had yielded a bountiful crop. When that crop was combined in the fall, tests indicated it would require extra drying in grain bins. Fortunately, years earlier Logan's dad had bought several grain bins, and they stood in an area behind the barn.

At harvest, various tests ascertain the amount of moisture in the beans. If the crop is collected before the beans are sufficiently dry, the crop is placed in storage bins, those owned by the farmer himself or through a local co-op. Heat is generated at the base of the bins and is then blown into those units to promote drying. Further tests indicate when enough moisture has been removed that mildew or mold will not develop. Too much moisture can cause the collection of beans to stick to the walls of the bin. After drying, those clumps of beans may fall, clogging the vents of the blower and causing the circulation of hot air to stop. A farmer, always making sure the blowers are shut down, then might climb down into the bins and try to remove those clogs. This exercise is extremely dangerous. The sequence of events that causes a farmer to be covered and subsequently smothered in the cascading of beans is one of the elements which qualifies farming as one of the top three most dangerous vocations.

On a Saturday in mid-October Leah and Logan had awakened to a morning that declared to them in no uncertain terms that summer was leaving and they should get it into their heads that winter would soon be blowing in. Logan loved harvest time, the cooling of the days and nights and the crispness of the mornings and always declared that the fall was his favorite season; however, Leah found he was prone to say the same about spring. She loved the Technicolor of the season but dreaded the message it brought each year ... the promise, or as she saw it, the threat, of the cold, ice, and snow that would soon be upon them.

The morning had started with a weak, anemic sun in a grey sky which had become greyer as the day progressed. Both Leah's brothers, Paul and Jim, were helping with the harvest that week-end. Jim had moved to Kansas, and Leah's older brother Paul worked in the family lumber yard. Her dad had been considering retiring, but just as Merrill Cummings had been reluctant to turn over the control of the farm to Logan, so was Ted Weeks reluctant to surrender control of the lumberyard to his son Paul. As a mother watches her child leave for its first day of school, as she watches the child go to college, or as she waves good-by at an airport to the child that departs for basic training, the relinquishing of control of a family's business to a son must be that difficult for a father.

Brother Jim had graduated from Iowa State University with a degree in electrical engineering. Moving to Wichita, Kansas, brought career opportunities in aerodynamics. He had made friends there and was thinking of asking a young lady to marry him.

Paul had attended two years at Iowa State, but after working several years in Des Moines, found that he, like Leah, wanted to be "home" in his small town. He had talked his dad into installing computers, allowing them to take a giant stride into the twentieth century. He had married, and the first Weeks grandchild was expected in February.

In the fall both brothers enjoyed harvesting the crops of corn and beans with their brother-in-law on his farm. Jim took a couple of vacation days during harvest season. Paul gave the reins back to his dad at the lumber yard, and all three young men reunited as a family fraternity. Overseeing all was Merrill Cummings, although he had become less vocal about how he would have done things than when he was running the show fifteen years before.

Leah fixed a lunch, which in farm terms was more accurately referred to as a noon dinner, a dinner of a hamburger casserole, salad, fresh bread still warm from the oven, and a pie from her own frozen peaches. The men had returned to their outdoor duties of combining beans, filling the farm wagons (one borrowed truck from a neighbor) and then filling the grain bins.

Tomato vines had all but died, and Leah the night before had pulled off the last of the red tomatoes. Most were small, and many were pock marked. The supply was not pretty but would do for homemade tomato juice and salsa.

The canning jars had been sterilized, and Leah was in the process of pushing the boiled fruit through a colander to make the juice itself when Jim came running into the house.

"Call 911! My cell phone's out!" he shouted. "Logan fell inside the grain bin. We got 'im out, but he's been smothered by the grain. He's still unconscious. It's bad, Sis. Get an ambulance out here. Quick!"

Leah would review the scene later and recall how composed she had been. It's been noted that a driver of a car can be side-swiped by another vehicle and not notice that his arm resting on the window frame had been amputated in that swipe until many minutes later. The words she heard did not fully register in her psyche until some time had passed.

Leah made the hasty call. Then without grabbing a jacket, she ran after Jim to the grain bins where Paul and Merrill were working over Logan. Logan was stretched prostrate on the ground, his face an awful blue-grey.

"Logan, Logan, she screamed. "Logan, please!" She was on her hands and knees bending over him.

"Move away, Sis, and give Paul room to work," Jim said in a quiet, deliberate voice as he pulled her away.

Leah stood and moved close to Logan's dad. The old gentleman had relinquished his spot to Paul and was standing motionless, staring at his son. Putting her hand through the crook of his arm, she felt him trembling. She squeezed the older man's arm and whispered, "Please, God. Don't let this be happening. Make him breathe."

Paul continued to perform CPR, and Jim from time to time would check for pulse at Logan's wrist. At one point Jim looked at Paul and said, "It's working. We've got a pulse here. Let me spell you for a minute."

Paul nodded. Jim knelt beside him and began the same rhythmic compressions. Paul sat back on his bent knees and watched Logan's face for signs of respiration. Slowly, some of the color began to climb under the collar of his jacket, up his neck and into his face. The eyes did not open, and no facial expression was seen.

In the analysis of time who's to say the length of fifteen or twenty minutes for that was the time needed for the ambulance to make its appearance from Glendale. In listening to an enchanting CD of music, in the serenity of watching an ocean tide embrace a shore, watching the spell binding flames in a fireplace, fifteen or twenty minutes would not be noticed, and, in fact, if noticed at all, would only know sadness in realizing those minutes had passed. To Leah those minutes were forever. Finally, the loud, irritating honking of an ambulance and the piercing screams of an accompanying police car were heard.

Paul ran to the barn yard gate and waved at the approaching vehicles. The driver maneuvered the ambulance into the barnyard where he spied the distressed family. Leah, still oblivious to the cold, remained huddled against her father-in-law, partly as a comfort to herself and partly to help steady him.

The driver and a muscular EMT quickly pulled a gurney from the back of the ambulance. A third young man in a short sleeved tee that allowed the exposure of tattoo-covered arms and neck ran with a black bag to the inert body on the ground. After checking for vitals, the men lifted Logan onto the gurney. Two of the EMTs jumped into the back of the ambulance and continued working over him. One technician immediately pulled off Logan's jacket and hooked him to machines. The third EMT, the apparent driver, was on the mobile phone, contacting the hospital in Glendale.

"We'll run with him to Glendale," he said when he had hung up. "Doctors can assess him there. Joe in the police car will run interference for us. We'll meet you in the emergency room."

After a short while the driver jumped back into the cab behind the wheel. The doors were closed, and the emergency vehicle headed very smoothly, and to Leah's mind, very slowly toward the barnyard gate. *"Far too slow,"* she fretted.

As the ambulance left the barnyard, the police car passed it and led the way, turning on its siren as it found the driveway.

"Leah, Merrill. Neither one of you is going to drive. You're riding with me," Paul yelled as he ran to his car. "Jim, you follow in Logan's pick up. We'll try to keep up as much as we can with the ambulance. Keys are still in the ignition."

At the hospital Logan's vitals were stabilized although he did not regain consciousness.

"Your husband is critical, but he's stable now. You know we can only do so much for him here. He has to get to a bigger hospital in Des Moines or to Iowa City," the doctor from the emergency room said. "We'll get things started here.

"Let's go to Des Moines. I know those hospitals better," Leah said, looking at Merrill for consensus.

"Then we'll make arrangements to life-flight him there. Let's get started on the paper work."

Suspecting rules were being broken, Leah insisted that she ride in the helicopter. Jim retrieved his car at his brother's home and picked up Logan's mother. A call had been made to her on the way to the hospital from Leah's cell phone, contained in the purse she had so hastily grabbed. They arrived at the hospital, and Jim assisted her to the emergency room. Hearing the news of the anticipated life-flight to Des Moines, the youngest brother filled his car with gas in preparation for the two hour trip that Logan's family would take in pursuit.

The helicopter landed at the medical center in Des Moines early evening, and the family convened there shortly after. Logan was settled in a room in the Intensive Care Unit. He was placed on a ventilator and other life support systems, and after only a few tests, it was determined he had suffered severe brain damage. Although life remained in his body, he did not awaken.

Chapter 10

Critical

Leah's legs trembled. The elevator doors opened onto the third floor, the coronary care unit. She walked a short distance, turned the corner into the large corridor, and passed through the dark green double doors and past the nurses' station. A stout nurse was seated at a computer, making entries from notes on her desk. A second nurse looked up, and with a look of recognition, smiled, and then returned her gaze to papers she was reading.

Leah walked further down the corridor, now with the back of her hand touching the cool pewter painted plaster. The weakness of her legs derived some strength as she sought support from the cold, unyielding structure of the walls. At the end of the hall, in an isolated bed, lay the comatose body of her husband.

Her arrival became more traumatic to her with each passing morning. In the first days of his comatose state she had entered his room with hope. As the days passed, though, she saw little, if any, change in his condition. She first had spent nights sleeping in a reclining chair, hoping there might be some new sign of awakening, and watching for any changes, even the flickering of an eyelid or the twitch of a finger that might occur in his being, anything that she could report to the nurses.

But each night became a routine for every other night. The nurses who arrived for duty at eleven exchanged notes and reviewed any changes of the patient, either his stats or new meds. In Logan's case, the updates were always short. Leah would lie in her lounge chair and listen with her eyes closed. The nurse assuming care at eleven would write her name on the chalk board tacked to the wall at the foot of his bed, declaring an impersonal, obscene intrusion into the privacy of Leah and Logan's lives. This assigned nurse each night, although appearing two and three nights consecutively, was never a person to Leah. Her appearance into the room on the occasions she made her rounds was always a shadowy, stealthy figure. A quarter century earlier, the figure might have been more noticeable in the dark as she would have appeared in a white dress uniform and would have even worn a white cap with a stripe of some varying width to identify the length and degree of her education. These nights the nurse's anonymity was less personal in the nondescript uniform of pajama-cut pants and generic fitting tunic. In the daylight the color would be a muted blue or green, but in the vague darkness of the hospital room, the uniform was even less appealing and almost sinister.

After a week in which no change occurred in Logan's physical or mental state, Leah realized that she was providing nothing positive in sleeping at his side in the lounge chair. On the one occasion when he had encountered a crisis in the intensive cardiac care unit, she had been forced from the room and told to go to the waiting room so the emergency team could function without her presence. Maybe she didn't need to hear the words spoken. Maybe she didn't need to see the grotesque procedures taken. She was summoned after Logan had been stabilized. Only then was she allowed to return to his room. Leah resigned herself to the conclusion that rather than spending seven twenty-four hour cycles a week at the hospital, she would be more effective to Logan's wellbeing by spending the night in a nearby hotel bed. She found she could return phone calls, wash by hand a few articles of clothing her parents and her brothers had delivered to her, and get some semblance of a night's sleep. She assumed if an emergency arose, she would receive a phone call, and the time she arrived at the hospital would probably coincide with the time she would have been allowed back into the room if she had stayed at the hospital.

Now, this morning, as she walked towards his room, she could feel the fear eroding her stomach. She swallowed, trying to dispel the rising nausea. Each morning there was no sign of his awakening and no word of progress from the notes of the night nurse. Last night the nurse from the second shift brought to her attention the reshaping and twisting of Logan's body into a fetal position with a reminder that this was not a good sign. Nobody gave her any hints of encouragement for his recovery.

Leah entered the last room at the end of the hall. When Logan had been transferred to this floor from the ICU, she had watched as they wheeled his mobile bed to the last room at the end of the hall, the room furthest from the nurses' station and the room furthest from the waiting room. She observed at the time, *"They're moving him away from everybody to be alone. They're giving up on him, and they're moving him to this far away room to die."*

Walking to the edge of his bed, she tightly clutched the rails which had been raised so he couldn't roll when he began his thrashing. "Good morning, Logan. Did you sleep well?" she whispered. "I'm back, and I brought with me a day of sunshine. When you wake up, we'll walk in it again. Just not today, my sweet warrior."

Some days Logan was enough awake from the depths of his coma to be aware of her voice. This morning, Logan's eyes opened as she spoke. As he moved his head toward her, the tube to the ventilator caught on his pajama tunic. The gaze of his open eyes moved to her face and then on past. But his head stopped in its turn and came back. This time as his head turned, it stopped. His eyes appeared to focus on her face. Then the eyes blinked. Slowly, the cracked lips turned into a smile. Leah's heart leaped, and tears were suddenly at the rims of her eyes. He had heard her voice and remembered it to be hers. Then he had given all the signs of seeing her. The smile that was directed to her face had surely been one of recognition. Nothing like this had happened since he had slipped into this comatose state. What awakening had transpired during the night and this morning? Something had happened that the nurses hadn't detected. But, then, maybe breakthroughs of comas weren't evident in all cases. Maybe a breakthrough in Logan's awakening wasn't easily detected by the robotic attention, or inattention, of the night nurse.

The smile lingered as long as four, maybe five seconds, and then slipped away, back into the blank countenance. But those four or five seconds were an unforgettable episode in Leah's eyes. His eyes closed, and the head returned to its usual passive state. Leah's legs, which had become stronger as she had entered his room, were once again weak and shaking. She steadied herself, turned, and met face to face the first shift day nurse.

"On, my Lord!" she whispered. "Did you just now come into the room? Did you see what happened? Did you see what he just did?" Leah could feel the tears dampen her lashes as she continued to speak. "I spoke to him when I came in, and he heard me. He recognized me. He actually saw me. I mean, he really did see me." She felt her chest would explode with new hope. "He's never done this before. This has to be a big step. He's never done this. Doesn't this mean he's waking up?"

The day nurse was one with whom Leah had bonded. Brenda Kingery had sat and talked with her earlier in the week and had told her of the bleakness of Logan's condition. Although she had provided comfort, at the same time she had explained the depth of Logan's coma and the slim chance he would awaken and, even at that, that his existence would have very little chance of normalcy.

Leah was not to be pulled down from her cloud. What had transpired was obviously a breakthrough in Logan's condition. No doubt. She had experienced incidents this week and last week when she knew Logan was aware of his surroundings. She had been advised to talk to him when she was near his bed. She touched his arms, his face, his hands. She combed his hair and wiped his face and lips with warm, moist wash cloths. Usually there was no response, but occasionally she knew there was a gap in the moss covered, very fuzzy wall around his mind, and she was allowed to step through. Whether it prompted a response or any awareness, the touching of his skin brought comfort to her. She played "This little piggy went to market, this little piggy stayed home…" with his toes. She rubbed his arms and legs with lotion, and rolling him slightly in his bed, she rubbed lotion on his back.

A daily routine involved playing with his fingers. From his folded hands she lifted his little finger and said to him, "This is your little finger, the pinky." She lifted the next finger and said, "This is your ring finger. This finger tells the world that you're married to me." Lifting the middle finger, she would say, "And this is your naughty finger." She hesitated briefly. He then raised his first finger in anticipation of her next directive. Leah laughed aloud and said, "And this is your power finger."

"You heard me and understood my words, didn't you? You're even awake enough to anticipate my next words and can lift your finger by yourself. Sweetie, you're getting better. Maybe tomorrow you'll wake, and you'll know me. Then I can take you out of this place, and you can come home."

The statement was entirely unrealistic. She had been told if Logan did awaken from his comatose state, his chances of returning home to a useful, functioning existence were extremely remote. Brenda had explained that going home would be an industrial-strength accomplishment. And in that thought just 'going home' was the achievement. She had warned her that he might not ever walk, that he might be confined to a wheelchair or even to a bed. He might speak; then again, maybe there would never be any dialogue. Maybe he could communicate by writing or by just nodding or blinking in response to her questions. Maybe he'd never communicate at all. Maybe he would never reach out to tease her with a pinch on her bottom or, in silliness, touch his tongue to the end of her nose, or even kiss the lids of her eyes.

Brenda had asked her last week to think about what she wanted for him and what she wanted from him. "When, or if, you take him home, what do you see for yourself? How will you handle his episodes of depression when he grows weary of his existence? And he will grow very weary of his existence. How will you respond to his episodes of anger when his depression turns to frustration? Will he yell at you? Will he throw things? Will he even hit out at you?"

Logan was not a small man. Her life would be entirely changed. Would she adapt? Could she adapt? Would she want to? What did she want for Logan? Granted, her world would change, but what about his world?

"I know I can take care of him. Good care of him," Leah bristled. "I work in a medical clinic in Glendale, and I've gathered some medical knowledge. I know I can learn to give shots. I mean how hard is that? I can change sheets on his bed even with him in it if I have to. And there's all kinds of home care classes I can take. I am trainable, you know, and I can do it."

"My God, how do people dismiss their vows?" She mused. *"In sickness and in health. It's not as though there's a choice. Do contemporary services encourage*

people to personalize their vows and leave that part out?
'Let me see, I promise to cherish you in health and some
light cases of flu, but if you get really sick, I'm out'ta
here?'"

Leah had taken Brenda's words to her room and
chewed on them that evening, but they were hard words to
swallow. When she had gone to the chapel that afternoon to
plead with God, and then again that night and every night
since, Leah had changed the words of her prayer. Instead of
"Please, Dear Lord, bring healing to Logan and let me
bring him home," this last week she had prayed, "Please do
whatever is best for Logan. I'll concede to your will. I want
to bring him home with me, but if his life would be
horrible, then please do whatever is best for him."

She had seen so many horrible experiences of pain
and anguish. When his chest filled with congestion, and the
nurses suctioned the mucus from his lungs, how he
struggled. *"Don't tell me he isn't aware of what they're*
doing." His eyes would widen, and he would grab at the
nurses' arms. Leah would leave the room when they
warned her they were going to lavage his lungs. Of course,
if he were awake from his coma, she assumed he would be
able to cough and keep his lungs clear.

The 'swan' had to be watched so the site would not become infected. The 'swan', a device implanted in the top of his chest, was an entrance which allowed meds to be fed into his system without searching for a vein each time a prescription was to be administered. How easily that opening became inflamed and sore. It was cleaned and observed with each administration. But Leah assumed that if Logan awoke from his coma, he would be able to swallow pills....if oral medication would even be needed. Yes, of course, they would be needed. There would be the blood thinner, probably medicine needed for blood pressure and maybe anti- seizure meds. She realized there might be medicines to guard against strokes or heart attacks. At least as much as her innocent mind would allow.

"When he wakes up," she told herself, *"there will be weeks, maybe even months of improvement required in the hospital before he'll be allowed to come home."* She knew it would be workable. It would be doable.

In her prayer to God last night, as she lay with her head on her pillow, she was still bargaining. "I'm asking that you do whatever is best for him, but, Lord, if you'll let him come home, with Your help I could learn to do whatever's needed to make him better, to make him well. It might take months, but I know if You help me, if he's not walking when he leaves the hospital, we could teach him to walk. He would talk to me, and we could get what he needed. If he doesn't get well enough to work the farm, we could sell it and move into town." A lot of conjecture passed over the pillow with Leah setting all the terms. Finally she had floated into a troubled sleep. A deep restful sleep had not occurred immediately after the accident or any of the subsequent nights at the hospital in the ICU waiting room.

Chapter Eleven

Talking to Brenda

Leah's face flushed with excitement and hope. Brenda was nothing if she wasn't logical. Although the nurse might be considered plump, she was by no means obese. Age had allowed her to make peace with her weight, and remembering a time when her figure was considered shapely, she decided her mother's heritage had locked in who she was now. She had been told she was part Cherokee, and she was proud of that. Perhaps her black hair would not show gray as soon as her 'pure' Caucasian peers. She had become a learned, experienced nurse and certainly not without compassion. Taking Leah by the hand, the older lady led her into the hall.

"Let's walk a minute." The cardiac unit waiting room was at the end of the hall, but a small room was connected to the nurses' station. Brenda entered the room and waved to Leah to have a seat in the straight-back chair.

Leah sat and looked around her. Some conversations we have, some realizations we come to, even those experiences absorbed by osmosis define us. Leah looked around at the walls of the small room. Units of five shelves lined two walls, shelves filled with packages of paper gowns, paper towels, rubber gloves, disposable masks. Shelves filled with plastic jugs of sterile water, packages of disposable, plastic tubing, necessary paper refills for all the devices that the nurses needed to attend the patients on that floor. The shelves held all the properties that would qualify the room as frigid.

Leah decided, *"No, a heater would be required to get it to a frigid state."* This was worse.

The table against the third wall gave the room the only hint of any responsibility in the participation of life. The table supported a large coffee maker. Beside that were stacks of Styrofoam cups, a tray with packets of sweeteners and cream substitutes, and a box of plastic spoons. An assortment of personal mugs stood with their handles to each other, appearing back to back, and seemingly showing as much disdain for each other as to the room itself. On a single shelf below this disarray were magazines, a few of medical content, several old issues of "People Magazine," a copy of a "Reader's Digest," and a recent issue of the "The Enquirer."

Leah watched as Brenda, pushing with one foot, rolled a three-legged stool over to her. She had filled two cups with coffee and now handed one to Leah. Then she perched herself in front of her.

Brenda looked at Leah, thinking to herself how this young face had become so tired in just a few weeks. It was the same tiredness she had observed marking the faces of so many loved ones of those patients who were profoundly ill. Spouses, children, parents of patients who have not responded well to treatment. As hospital care is extended and no signs of improvement are seen, family members become more and more weary. Especially true were those cases in which a patient lay in a comatose state or in a state of non-communication, even though those patients may be well aware of their environment and of happenings around them.

Brenda leaned forward and took one of Leah's hands in her own. "Sweetie, I brought you down here so we could talk. Just the two of us, and I didn't want Logan to hear us. And, yes, we are both aware that sometimes he does tune us in."

She released Leah's hand and, curling her ankles and feet around the legs of the stool, she leaned back. "I love my job as a nurse, but there are parts of it that I wish didn't belong. I love the feeling I get when I can administer to a patient and see that patient respond and show signs of getting well. I love what happens to that patient. I love the hope that sits in on the edge of his bed and fills that room. I love watching his family get well right along with him. I see them going from clasping their hands together with worry and crying to laughing and making plans to live again when that patient they love so much is on the mend. It's all about coming to life again."

She sighed and continued, "And then, again, sometimes I see families who bicker and blame each other. Those are the ones I wonder if that patient is really better off getting well. You'd like to ask him if he really wants to go back out into that storm."

Brenda hesitated and watched Leah, then went on. "But, Leah Girl, there's parts of my job I really don't like. In fact…that I hate. And those are the times when I don't see a patient improving. Those are the times I can almost open a text book, read a page from a patient's daily chart, and it'll be the same as a page in that manual. I'm talking about a chapter in the text when the prognosis says the patient won't get well."

Continuing on, Brenda said, "I'm not saying Logan isn't getting better, but I'm asking you not to be too encouraged by the signs you saw this morning. But if he does get well, it's going to be a long, slow road to recovery. And I won't even start to define 'recovery'."

Listening intently to Brenda, Leah's shoulders, which had been squared with the world when she sat down, now slumped. She said, "But you don't know how each case will be. I've been reading some of the magazines from the waiting room, and yesterday afternoon I read of the case of a rodeo rider who had taken a kick in the back of the head and then been dragged around the arena. This young kid had been in a coma, and then one day he just opened his eyes and was pretty much okay from then on. I mean, he was said to be way out. What makes you think that can't happen to Logan?"

Brenda thought a moment and then answered, "Without knowing about your bronc rider, I can't say for sure. If he were kicked in the head or stomped on by a horse or thrown hard against the railings, maybe he had some serious brain swelling. I'm not minimizing an injury like that, but that wouldn't have had the same consequences on someone as an event like Logan's. Your husband's heart stopped when he was smothered in that grain bin. We know there was no blood circulation to his brain for maybe as long as nine or ten minutes. No oxygen. During that time, great damage was destroying his brain. I can't tell you what was destroyed. Will he come back? There's some small chance that he will, but, Leah, I'm not seeing any signs of it."

Leah sat quietly, listening. Trembling, she sipped on her cup of coffee. Brenda continued. "What you saw this morning seems so promising to you, but I don't think you can see it as a big step forward. The last four days we've seen Logan posturing into a fetal position. This isn't good. We're fighting some spiking fevers, could be Thalamic Storms, which is what happens when the Thalamus mass goes out of whack. High temperatures like he experienced yesterday afternoon are like frying his brain. That's why we put him on the ice sheets."

Brenda watched Leah's hands. Leah finished the last swallow of coffee. As she listened to Brenda, her fingernails made a pattern of indentations around the lip of the Styrofoam cup. Brenda had been on duty six of the last ten days Logan had been on her floor. As good nurses often do when they care for very ill patients, they become emotionally attached to the patients' families and loved ones. Brenda had tried in the past to divorce herself from those attachments but for the most part found it couldn't be done. There was no way she could have remained distant from this family of Logan's. In particular she had bonded with his wife. Studying her now, Brenda noticed how frail Leah appeared to be. Fragile was certainly not a characteristic she would have labeled her if she had known her before the accident, but at this moment she looked quite breakable.

Leah's short blonde hair was brushed away from her face. Brenda suspected the color was natural. Leah had no need for camouflage or cover-up. She used little make-up, and at this moment her lips were bare of lipstick. Her pale blue turtleneck sweater added no color to her countenance. At any other time the soft blue would have made her appear girlish with an air of gentility. Now it only whispered of her vulnerability. Jeans were clean and starched and even pressed, probably the continuation of years of habit.

Leah finally looked up. Her lashes were damp, but she was composed.

"I appreciate your input, and I appreciate your caring enough to level with me. I know I can't do much in this except to pray that Logan'll come around, although last night, I have to tell you I did change my request. I asked God to do what is best for Logan. Of course, I'm hoping that "best" is being home with me."

Changing the tone of her conversation, she asked Brenda, "What do you think happens in their world when they're in a coma? In the article I read last night, when the rodeo rider was interviewed after he woke up, he said he had sometimes been aware of sounds and conversations around him. He said he remembered hearing the doctors talking to his wife, and he had heard a vase break when it had been dropped on the floor. I know Logan heard me this morning, and he's heard me other times. Do you think they're trapped in a different dimension? And all the time, or just part of the time?"

Brenda leaned forward again on her rolling stool.

"Sometimes I think when they're really deep and away from us that maybe they're on a little cloud way off somewhere and talking to God. Who knows? So often when they wake up, they say they don't remember most of it. Usually they remember little smatterings. Wouldn't it be wonderful if Logan already knows what's happening and what will happen, and he's at peace with all of it? That he's okay with it all?"

Leah stood up and pushed a tendril of hair behind her ear. Her fingers had stilled their nervous dance around the crumbling lip of the cup. Looking into the kind eyes of Brenda, she smiled and said, "I like that. I think I'll hold onto that thought. Thank you. And thank you for trying to carry me through this." She stepped away from the kind nurse but then turned, walked back, and wrapping both arms around her neck, hugged her tightly.

Leah dropped the ratty cup into the waste can and walked out of the room. She walked through the nurses' station and back into the hall and then slowly into Logan's room. He lay on his back, sleeping still. She watched as the ventilator pumped its steady, hissing beat. A hanging plastic bag neared empty, a plastic bag of whatever. If she needed to learn what and its purpose and how much, she knew she could do that. She would also learn the when and the why of it.

Passing a table filled with cards and three small vases of pink carnations, red carnations, and roses, she walked to the far side of the bed and to the window ledge. She pushed the ON button of the CD player. The voice of Garth Brooks began. "I've got friends in low places, where the whiskey…" She tried to choose fun tunes that he would recognize and, lately, some Christian tunes. She had recently become acquainted with the music and lyrics of Michael W. Smith. She knew Logan would find that music comforting. She certainly did. And she decided some of the music in the room was to strengthen and calm her.

Leah walked again to the side of his bed. She began a ritual which now occurred daily. She rubbed his arms and legs, played with his fingers and talked to him. She sat in the chair beside his bed when she wasn't sitting on the edge of his bed beside him. Occasionally it seemed to her, but actually on a much regimented time schedule, a nurse would appear to check vitals and listen for congestion in his lungs. Two nurses came in to change his bedding and to give him a sponge bath. Leah shaved his face and brushed a dry hair cleaner into his sandy, brown hair. She was more and more aware of his thinning hair and knew how he hated that loss. She combed through the hair, lifting his head in her hand as she combed with the other, talking to him always. Brenda stopped in about mid-morning as much to check on her as to check on Logan.

A little before noon neighboring friends from the farm stopped to see him. Since conversation was only with her, they suggested she join them for lunch in the hospital cafeteria. Although others remarked at the bland food in the hospital cafeteria, Leah had not found it to be all that unappetizing, although she often satisfied any hunger, if she noticed hunger at all, with a bag of microwave popcorn which she popped in the visitor's waiting room, or a Coke, a bag of chips and a package of Lorna Doones from the vending machine by the elevator doors.

Chapter Twelve

Good Byes

Leah had a sit-down lunch at a cafeteria table. She found herself relaxing at a square, teak-wood table facing her neighbors. What should have qualified as an everyday dining routine had become foreign to her these past weeks. Today she savored her cheesy potato soup, appreciating small bites of ham. As her neighbors plied her with questions about Logan's current status and prognosis, she enjoyed half a chicken salad sandwich. She noted to herself how pleasant it was to be away from Logan's room. At the same time, she felt a tug of guilt at the top of her stomach that she should be so content being away from him when the daytime hours were all she allowed herself to be in this facility. Nevertheless, she leisurely spooned the chocolate pudding, enjoying its smooth texture and relishing the fact that she could be so lazy. Feeling like a very small child, she needed not to chew; just spoon, savor, and swallow.

Eventually, conversation slowed, and Leah's neighbors promised they would continue to watch for any curious activities around her farm. With words of assurance, "Now promise to let us know if we can do anything to help," and "You and Logan are in our prayers," they walked with her to the elevator doors. Hugs, needed hugs, were exchanged with both Wilma and Dean, and she entered the elevator that would again take her to the third floor. She waved goodbye as the doors closed and promised to let them know of any improvements in Logan's condition as they happened.

The elevator was surprisingly empty at this noonday. She made the short ride to the third floor, observing she would have benefited by walking the steps and noted to herself she would do that the next time she ate in the cafeteria.

The Otis lift gently stopped. The doors slid open, and as Leah stepped out, the small, closet like room quickly filled with a family of five, chattering and comparing observations of their loved one's condition. The doors closed on their voices, and Leah made her way once again to Logan's room at the end of the hall.

She stood at the side of his bed, watching the ventilator breathe for him, listening to its steady pump and hiss. He had had another spike in his temperature, and the nurses had spread an ice mattress under his body again. Curling her fingers around the railing of his bed, she steadied herself as a wave of weakness spread downward from her shoulders. But the weakness was more than that. Suddenly she was so tired she felt she could not breathe air into her lungs and then expel it. If she could see the gases she was inhaling, she was sure they would have been colored a dark gray hue, a color of despair.

Leah choked back a sob that had swollen in her throat. She walked to the far side of Logan's bed and then sat down in the straight chair between his bed and the window. Leah reached across Logan's chest and took his hand which was now cold and purplish from the icy cold of the mattress. She nudged her chair closer to the side of his bed and brought his hand to her breast. As she held his hand between her own warm palms, she began to cry. The hope from that morning now came crashing down and lay in a pool at her feet. Draining down into the pool were the plans she had conjured in these last several days. Maybe she wouldn't be bringing him home. Maybe at this point of consciousness he wouldn't be cognizant of his surroundings, that she would be able to care for him. She allowed herself to visualize a state of being in which he had no control, and Logan had always been one in control. He was a proud man. To live his existence immobile and in a wheel chair – he would hate that. In time, maybe he would grow to hate her. To not spend his day working and achieving would be unbearable for him. He would know no sunshine. And because of his despair, there would be no sunshine for her.

Holding his hand tightly in hers, Leah continued to softly cry. Finally there were no more tears. She held his hand in her hand and leaned her head on the stiff-backed chair. With the other hand, she pulled a soft tissue from her jeans pocket and wiped her tears and runny nose. Then she closed her eyes.

She wakened to see Brenda taking Logan's temperature and charting his blood pressure and pulse. Brenda left the room but returned quickly with an aide. The two began turning Logan, removing the icy mattress beneath him. Leah noticed his back and buttocks and legs were mottled and purplish from the arctic cold of the mattress.

The caring nurse asked, "How are you doing this afternoon? Is there anything you need, and, by the way, did you get any lunch?"

She was charting Logan's temperature spikes and added, "I'll tell the doctor that the ice mattress brought the spiking temps down, but it certainly hasn't stopped them.

And they certainly don't seem to be lessoning. The doctor hasn't made rounds yet today, but he should be here before I finish my shift."

When Brenda left, Leah found the remote and turned on the TV above the foot of Logan's bed. There had been a time when her ears and eyes had sponged the dire events from "Days of Our Lives," but today none of the story registered. Maybe a hundred years ago she would have lost an hour of her existence in a nonsensical, nonrealistic world of a soap opera. She might at some time have languished in a tale that took her from her reality, but today she didn't dare slip away. Her world now consisted of this hospital room with its rasping, blinking machines and its solitary bed with Logan curled up.

The tale on the TV ended, at least for the day. Leah turned off the television and walked again to the end of the hall to the vending machine. She satisfied the hunger of the mercenary machine and heard the clonk of the falling Coke. She stopped in the visitors' waiting room, picked up remnants of the morning paper and continued back down the hall to Logan's room. Passing the nurses' station, she noticed the day nurses were briefing those who were checking in for the evening shift. Brenda was conversing with a young nurse who was studying a patient's chart and noting information on the computer screen.

"Probably telling her of Logan's day," Leah mused.

The afternoon nurse was one Leah had met a week earlier, but who had not been in attendance this week. Leah had noted at their meeting a week ago that she must have been a new graduate. Remembering her as Amy, Leah was struck again at her youth. She had not rid herself of her first impression that this was not a magna cum laude graduate. She didn't give the impression of being among the top half of her peers. Leah was struck with the notion of *"Hope she's not the General Custer of her class."*

Continuing on to Logan's room, she laid her newspaper in the Lazy Boy chair and walked into the restroom. When she returned, Amy was writing notes in Logan's file.

"Good afternoon, Leah." Amy looked up as Leah stepped to her side. "I took some vacation time, and I was hoping Logan might have wakened by now. Doesn't seem to be much progress according to Brenda and these doctors' notes. I'm sorry. This isn't the most comforting place in the world, is it?"

Leah felt her appraisal of Amy softening.

"No, it's not like spending a week in Disney World. I had hoped Logan would be showing more signs of waking up by now, too. This morning when I came in, I was sure I was seeing such great improvement, but there's been nothing since then. I mean nothing. But then, I imagine Brenda brought you up to date on everything. In fact, this day has been dreadfully long. If anything, as the day has gone on, it seems he's drifted further away from me."

As they compared notes, Brenda stepped into the room. "I'm checking out, Little Girl. I won't be in tomorrow or Friday so I wanted to tell you that I'll probably see you when I get back on Saturday." Leah looked at her and saw Brenda's face smile. "Besides taking care of Logan, why don't you see about taking care of you? Hear me?"

"Thanks for your words this morning. I've thought about them a lot today. Yes, I'm sure we'll still be here on Saturday. It's supposed to be nice, so enjoy your days off." Leah wished Brenda weren't leaving, and she especially wished she would be here these next several days.

Brenda gave her shoulder a squeeze, turned and left the room. Amy finished jotting notes and left also. Their intrusion had lasted only moments, but Leah was left feeling even more alone. She had planned to sit and read the morning's paper, but suddenly she desperately needed to feel the peace of the chapel.

She left Logan's room and walked along the corridor to the elevator. The doors opened to an empty compartment, and she stepped in. The first floor button lit up as the lift started its ride down. A stop was made to let a young couple on, and then the doors opened on to the main floor. As she exited the elevator and turned to the chapel, Leah felt a keen sense of panic. If she were a small child, she would have run to the shelter of the chapel, but composure owned her, and she slowly walked to its heavy doors. She stepped inside and saw she was its only visitor.

"Good," came the whisper from her lips. "I need this time with You, just You and me."

The deep, red padded seat of a bench at the side of the small altar welcomed her as she sank onto it. Folding her hands in the lap of her jeans, she looked steadily at small burning candles and acknowledged the statuette of Mary, mother of Christ. The sense of peace that permeated the sanctuary was calming and healing to anyone who settled there and who had come with a spiritual need. Leah lowered her chin and rested. For a few minutes the silence was heavy on her shoulders, heavy but comforting like her grandma's old, heavy quilt on a chilly evening. In the silence was a communication between her and a powerful, healing Spirit.

"Please, help me accept what's in store for Logan and me. You have this all figured out, don't You?" she whispered. "Aren't you going to let him stay with me? How can I be here without him?"

There! She had spoken the words aloud. She was asking, facing the possibility that he might not continue in this life with her.

"Help me feel the strength I need." The prayer wasn't for Logan now; it was for her. "There's no way I can do this without You." Then she was silent.

She continued to rest and to reflect on what was becoming evident to her. No further dialogue was necessary. She remained seated four or five minutes more, then rising, she turned and walked back out the wooden, double doors.

She slipped into Logan's room and saw the sunshine had slid further down the red brick walls on the west side of the building. Late afternoon had brought its grey, dusty film which hung in the corners, draped across the chairs and over Logan's bed.

She seated herself again in the Lazy Boy chair beside Logan's bed and awoke the light from the lamp at its side. Late afternoon, almost evening. She finally could begin to read the morning's Register but was distracted to see Amy enter the room.

Amy checked one of the drip bags, then checked again Logan's pulse. She studied the readings on the monitors and made more notes in his chart.

"Why are you checking on him so soon?" Leah asked, "You checked just a few minutes ago."

Amy finished her notes. Then, walking over to Leah who had risen from her chair to allow her to replace one of the bags, Amy lowered her voice and spoke softly.

"He's not doing well now, Leah. His respiration is shallower, and his pulse is slower and weaker than it was 20 minutes ago and even less than before that. I'm going to call Dr. Baker and your general practitioner, Dr. Anderson. They need to know of any changes. I don't think there's much they can do, but they need to be notified."

The roller coaster Leah had boarded that morning rocketed nose downward again.

"What's causing him to be weaker? Of course. Call both doctors." She heard her own voice and was surprised at its calm. She thought she was screaming, but it didn't sound loud at all. "Surely one of them will have an idea of something they can do. Maybe if they shock the heart, that will make it stronger."

Amy shook her head and said, "I'm sure that won't be of any help." She hesitated, and then added as she left the room, "But maybe."

The frightening words Amy had spoken brought an urgency to call Logan's parents. They had traveled to Des Moines every day the first weeks, but when the days brought no changes that they could see, they came only every other day. She had promised she would call them if Logan's condition changed even the slightest. The call was made from her cell phone in the isolation of the normally busy waiting room. She didn't want Logan to hear the words that his condition was worsening.

Leah stood again at the edge of the bed.

"Logan, please don't go away," she whispered. She leaned close over him. "Please be strong again."

The late afternoon became evening, and Amy and the other nurses kept their timely vigils. Dr. Baker stopped as well as Dr. Anderson.

Dr. Baker said quietly, "Logan's heart, as tired and damaged as it is, is wearing out. Shocking the heart won't do any good." He stayed a few minutes and then left, saying, "I'll stop in again after I've finished my rounds. I'll stop before I leave the hospital."

Leah was left alone with Logan and still trying to wrap her mind around the finality of Dr. Baker's words when Dr. Anderson stopped by. He had been notified of Logan's weakening state and had come to the hospital as soon as he was finished with his afternoon office patients. Picking up the straight chair by the window, he brought it around the bed and placed it next to the Lazy Boy. He motioned her to sit, then settled himself beside her chair.

In a very soft voice, barely audible to Leah, he began.

"There's just nothing more we can do now, Leah. Doctors have only so much knowledge and intuition. Then we're brought to a point where we no longer have a say. Logan is in God's hands now. We're watching the last page in Logan's story being written. Sometimes when I've been witness to this, I think I can feel Him close to us. There's another presence here." Dr. Anderson held her hands in his and watched her.

"I need to step out to the nurses' station. I'll be right back."

When he was gone, Leah rose again. She lowered the railing on Logan's bed and sat on its edge.   Holding   his hand in hers, she said, "Logan, if you hear my voice, squeeze my hand." She waited and held her breath. Then, very gently, she felt the pressure of his fingers encircling her hand. She slowly exhaled. "Logan, I love you."

Then again, "I love you."

And again, "I love you."

Unexpectedly, she again felt the pressure of his fingers encircling her hand.   With tears climbing to the brims of her eyes, she leaned back on the bed and pillow so she could lie down beside him. She pulled his arm to the side and away from his torso, being careful not to pull at the needles poking into his arm. Then she snuggled into his hospital clad chest. Putting her arms around him and hugging him tight, she lay close to him, noticing that his body felt much cooler next to hers. As she listened, she noticed the hissing of the respirator and the beeping of the monitors had slowed.

She wasn't aware of the presence of Amy or Dr. Anderson in the doorway, nor did she see the shadow from the hallway light of Dr. Baker. She heard only the slowing sounds of the machines in the room, and she felt the coolness of Logan's body. She raised herself to her elbow and kissed Logan's lips.

Leah sobbed and kissed his cheek. With that kiss, she felt the salt water taste of a tear. Later, she wondered if the saltiness had been a tear from Logan's eyes or if the tear was her own.

Then the room was silent. Only the ventilator could be heard. The steady quiet of a flat line. No hiss. No beep. Leah lay quietly.

A hand on her shoulder told her that her time alone with Logan was over. Dr. Anderson said, "Leah, he's gone." He helped her sit up and then with his stethoscope, the good doctor listened to Logan's chest.

"There's no expression of life. Amy, record the time is 6:13."

Leah was transfixed in another world, in another dimension. Later she remembered thinking, *"This is it? He'll never hug me? He'll never kiss me again?"*

Then thoughts that made no sense.

"Where did Dr. Anderson get that stupid looking tie?"

"Why does he comb over his hair like that?"

"I wonder if anyone will call Brenda and let her know."

"What will happen to me? Half of me is gone. The best half of me is gone."

Part III

A Promise Kept

Chapter Thirteen

A Growing Friendship

If April's sunshine and longer days brought an awakening of Leah's soul, then Stranger provided it with comfort and purpose. His presence, which had not been solicited, became a welcome addition to her hours at home. Each night when she drove into the garage from her work at the clinic, he stood like a sentry at the doublewide door. In fact, it wasn't unusual that he greeted the car at the entrance to the driveway.

Leah made a series of calls to neighbors inquiring about ownership or even knowledge of her four-legged friend and then informed her co-workers at the clinic. No one knew anything of a dog like Stranger. He had made himself at home, and she made no attempt to rid him from her life.

At first she was adamant as he continued to set up residence with her that he would not be allowed to stay in the house. He was a very large dog, and besides, "I'm not cleaning dog hair off my furniture and carpeting. I don't need it." When she was away from the house at work, Stranger apparently spent much of his day in the gazebo.

One night after Stranger had been at the farm a little more than a week, as Leah returned to her darkened house from being in her garden, Stranger followed her to the porch but stopped at the back door.

Leah stepped inside, switched on the kitchen light, and said, "You can come in and watch TV with me, but you can't get on the furniture." She continued, "When I go to bed, you go back outdoors." When bedtime came, perhaps she forgot her directive. He stayed the night. After Leah dismissed the light in her bedroom, she heard him pad softly into her room, then lay quietly on the floor at the side of her bed. She felt a great comfort when she awoke later in the night and heard his soft snore.

The morning alarm sounded, and Leah opened her eyes. The large dog still lay on the floor beside her bed. The sound of her stirring brought a thump of his furry tail on the carpet. She sat up in her bed, swung her feet from under the light covers, and laid them gently on top of the big watch dog there. Stranger lifted his head and looked at her.

"You're actually grinning, aren't you?" Leah smiled. "And you think you made a coup de maitre last night, don't you? Working yourself into the house for the night. Sleeping beside my bed. And come to think of it, you didn't even go out to potty before you went to bed here, did you?" Leah enjoyed the presence of having a living being to talk to first thing in the morning.

She brushed her teeth, gargled and dried her mouth, taking note that she was being observed. "Come on. Let's put you outdoors so you can do your 'business'. At least you're not standing there cross legged."

Stranger strolled slowly behind her as she shuffled to the back door and held it open. "You're not a ball of fire in the morning, are you?" she said. "Maybe you're like me. You do better as the day goes on."

So began a pattern. From "I don't need a dog in the house," to a happy acceptance of a deepening friendship enjoyed by both parties. As the days passed, Leah was surprised that Stranger seemed to have an innate sense of time and an awareness of the day of the calendar. He seemed to be aware of week-end days. She awoke one morning and without moving her head could sense him lying on the floor beside the bed. His eyes were open, and he watched her, waiting for her awakening. He allowed her to sleep into the morning. He seemed to appreciate her desire for uninterrupted rest.

Not only did Leah stop asking the history of her new pet, she dreaded that anyone might someday know about him or ever declare their ownership. Stranger had found a home and someone who needed him.

Chapter Fourteen

Experiencing Grief

In the year that followed Logan's death, Leah felt she had emotionally fallen to the bottom of a well. To be acquainted with grief is an experience that to know it, it must be lived. Books are written, songs are sung, operas are composed, loved ones are consoled, but to understand grief, one must personally walk through it. And just when the journey appears to be ending, the monster alien lashes out its tentacles and pulls the suffering one back into its lair.

Leah cried. And when she didn't cry, she couldn't allow herself to smile or imagine being happy. Then the grief had to step aside for guilt. *"Why didn't I kiss him after lunch that day? Why didn't I tell him I loved him more often?"* How could she allow herself to smile and laugh out loud? Never! *"The best part of me is gone,"* she wept. *"What's to smile about? Happiness was with Logan, and that will never happen again."*

Leah's job at the medical center was the means of making sure she continued to live. Each morning, after a night of wakefulness, she brushed her teeth and showered.

She methodically chose clothes that became looser as the months passed and her weight decreased. At the clinic she lost herself in medical charts, insurance papers and insurance laws, work schedules and employee payrolls. Her job was more than tedious paper work on which she applied her paralyzed mind. It was a community of people who cared about her and watched over her. She noticed the nurses and the office personnel made a point sometime every morning to poke their heads through the doorway and greet her. More so than before. Somebody each day asked her to join them at lunch. Leah had always been included, but noticing the extra attempts to comfort her helped heal her and made her heart smile.

Several weeks after Logan's funeral, a package had arrived in the mail. Opening it, Leah had found a beautiful, blank journal. The inscription on its first page had read, "For your eyes only..." and was from Logan's nurse, Brenda Kingery. Working at the medical center and taking care of her home, now accompanied by Stranger, motivated her to live, but the catharsis of her grief was in the filling of that journal and, later, others. Each night Leah sat in her bed, still on the same side she had always slept, and wrote in the book with its lined, empty pages.

For several weeks, Leah had neither energy nor motivation to put pen to paper. She felt no need or desire to write. She reasoned, *"My mind is nothing but mush. There's nothing to say."* But after a month, Leah began to write. At first the day's memories were one page, if that. Soon there were more, and she found that she was writing three and four pages under the gaze of the night light on her headboard. Often when she began writing, the force of her pen would be light. Then the ink became heavier and darker, and the writing came faster and faster as the words and the grief fell out onto the paper. Often, too, she would close her journal and feel a sense of relief before she switched off her lamp.

Eventually, looking back over the pages she had written, Leah began to see some healing. The more recent pages were less tormented, less full of despair. She began noting plans and goals that she would do tomorrow, or next week, or next month. She wrote of those tasks she would be doing alone. She, unknowingly and unnoticed, began making plans for a future. She began to heal.

Leah had been given advice by both her parents and Logan's parents. "Don't make any major decisions regarding your life, unless an emergency, for at least a year." Logan had died in the fall a short time before the end of October. Thanksgiving and then Christmas had been almost impossible. New Year's Eve followed, but she was too numb to notice much. Friends whom Logan and she had always met for celebration had called but said apologetically that they understood if she didn't want to join them. As more time passed, she felt less and less a part of their world even though her love for those couples never diminished.

The worst and most hurtful holiday, though, was Valentine's Day. Deliberately, Leah had driven to Des Moines to shop and to be by herself. She had spent the fourteenth of February shopping at a mall. At one point she stood on the top level of the two story structure and looked over the railing at the busy people, walking, window gazing, and shopping below her. Tears came flooding to her eyes as she noted that everyone, and she saw no exceptions, was part of a couple. Furthermore, most of the couples were holding hands. She stood silently, watching, allowing the tears to slide quietly down her cheeks.

"How can everyone be so happy? Don't they know, can't they see, my world is gone? Doesn't anyone care?" Besides missing her husband, she was acutely aware that the rest of the world had not changed. The world was totally oblivious to her and her aloneness. Only her

universe had changed, and that made no difference at all as the planet continued its elliptical trip around the sun. Not only was Logan gone, but she felt truly and absolutely alone.

Leah stood quietly, acknowledging and gradually accepting the finality of her past life. Finally, she walked to an ice cream specialty shop and ordered a small, generic vanilla cone. Sitting at the table in the food court, she slowly licked the cone and watched the people as they passed. She picked up her packages and walked to her car, crying on her trip home. This year she had not chosen a special Valentine's card that said just the right words. Usually she read at least a dozen cards before she found the one that said exactly what she wanted to say, and even at that, she would always add her own words to tell him what he meant to her. She also missed the card from him that wouldn't be there. Not this year. The day commemorating St. Valentine came and went but proved to be a day of some new acceptance, a new gradual revelation.

Chapter Fifteen

Sweet Spring

Spring came with its promise of a new life. Leah had no desire to leave the farm. The understanding had been clear that Logan would inherit the farm from his parents, and his sister Sarah, who wanted no part of rural Iowa, would receive a settlement equal to the value of the land. Sarah had moved to Austin and married a Texan. For her, Iowa was only a place to visit. In the years they had made the farm their home, Logan and Leah had split income from the farm with his parents. They had made improvements on the house and improved the machinery and livestock. Merrill Cummings told Leah she could live in the house as long as she wanted, the rest of her life if she so pleased. She was the widow of their only son, and even though no grandchildren resulted from that union, Leah was important to them not only because she was Logan's choice, but because she was their choice as well.

Arrangements were made to rent the land to a young neighboring couple, Simon and Nancy Turner, on a crop/share arrangement. Most of the cattle were sold shortly after Logan's death except for a few choice cows, Leah's Annie being on that short list that was held back. The young man tended those few cows and a prize bull, and for his tending the small herd, he would keep half the new calves as a start for his own small herd.

April rains and longer, warmer days inspired Leah to plant her own small garden again. It was the returning to a structured life, a time to look forward again, to plan, to make arrangements for a tomorrow. As she planted her tomato plants, her peppers and onions, her cucumbers and zucchini, she pictured canning juice again, making salsa and pickles. Watching the seeds develop into plants, the blossoms appear on her tomato vines, and the vines spread were as nourishing to her soul as any vitamin supplements or months long sessions of grief counseling. She began to live again.

Weekly therapy was provided in the mowing of her lawn on her old Wheel Horse tractor. Often she had time to mow after she arrived home from work, but her favorite time to mow the more than acre yard was on Saturday morning. And the spring after Logan's death had presented Saturdays that were created just for Leah's mowing. If rain had fallen Friday evening, Saturday morning would be clear, if not always sunny. And if rain were to continue that week-end, it always seemed to hold off until she had sheared the lawn of its long, green locks.

Logan had disconnected the tractor's battery the previous fall and had set it on old newspapers and an old throw rug on the cement basement floor. The last week of April Leah had carried the battery back out to the tool shed, set it under the hood of the faded red Wheel Horse, and connected it to the motor. She added fresh gas and climbed onto the seat. Pulling on the choke, she held her breath and turned the key.

"Grrr, grrr, grrr," Then finally a huge cough, and the mower begrudgingly acknowledged another spring. Leah smiled, pushed in the choke, and drove the lawn tractor out of the shed. Turning in the seat, she looked over her shoulder and saw Stranger standing at the door of the shed. He took several steps as though to follow her but changed his mind and directed his path to the gazebo. There he would wait and watch her as she mowed.

Leah lowered the mower deck and began the pattern around the yard she had mowed the years before. Each week she changed the course of the trail. The rusty, old tractor was noisy and though it was called a Wheel Horse, it could never be mistaken as a Race Horse. Logan had always laughed when he said it was good that they mowed at least an acre because an acre was needed to turn it around. But in spite of its noise, the fact that it ran on its own sweet schedule and that it refused to make sharp turns, it started consistently and always cut evenly a wide sixty inch swath.

Leah bumped gently in the large tractor seat that would easily have accommodated the hind portion of a large man. After mowing the front yard and the shallow ditch there, she steered the tractor towards the barnyard. She drove to the gate and stopped the tractor. In the barnyard stood Annie, now a full grown heifer who had been bred in the fall. Preferred time for calving was spring, but Annie's calf wouldn't arrive until summer. Leah walked to the fence and called to her.

"Hey, my pretty black faced girlfriend," she cooed. "I haven't had a chance to talk with you for such a long time."

Annie watched her, and as Leah began walking toward the fence, Annie sauntered towards her. "Oh, you are the princess, aren't you? You're growing into a big girl. I guess you're thinking about being a new mama, aren't you? Uh huh, you'll make a good little mommy."

Leah leaned against the fence as Annie poked her very big and very wet nose through the wooden railings.

Leah scratched the heifer's forehead and rubbed her ears. The two ladies were quiet, appreciating the bond between them. A third party appeared quietly at their side. He seemed to be aware of and was quite comfortable with the relationship between the two ladies. Leah had watched as Stranger had made himself known to some of the cattle but had noted a kinship between him and Annie. He sat on his haunches, watching as they reconnected and observed the reversal of roles as the young heifer became the nurturer to the sad widow. After a few minutes of rubbing the bristly hair along Annie's face and neck, Leah bid her adieu and returned to her Saturday morning mowing.

Leah finished her bumpy ride on the tractor, hosed it off and drove it back into the tool shed. She sprayed Round-Up at the base of the trees and at the base of the fence posts so she wouldn't have to trim each week with the weed eater. It had been a morning of nourishment, and Leah finished in time to fix herself a late lunch and sat down to rest.

*   *   *   *   *   *   *

Later that evening but before dark, an older, well-maintained car pulled into her driveway, and Leah watched as her father-in-law slowly stepped out. Without knocking at her door to make his presence known, he walked from the drive to the gazebo in the back yard. Standing at her back door, she watched as he wearily sat down facing the pond. She took two tall glasses from a shelf in the kitchen cupboard, filled them with sun tea and ice, and walked the distance to the gazebo and to her guest. As she stepped inside, she noticed he had already been joined by Stranger. She sat beside the older man and handed him one of the glasses. For several minutes they both sat in silence.

Mr. Cummings drank from the glass and then looked at her. "Sometimes I just want to come out here and be where he was. I didn't tell Rachel I was coming. I try not to be sad in front of her."

"You come out whenever you want. This is your home, after all. And don't be afraid of being sad in front of me." She put her hand through his arm and kissed his shirt sleeve at the shoulder. "I couldn't have a better mother and father-in-law than you and Rachel. But, then, why not? You're responsible for Logan." She squeezed his arm.

Both the old man and the young woman were quiet, gazing at the green mottled water of the pond and watching the shadows from the trees lengthen.

Finally, Logan's father spoke. "I've been so fortunate to raise a son and a daughter with nary a problem. I guess I wasn't surprised to see my little girl marry and leave the farm. A farmer's wife wasn't what she was etched out to be. No, I guess I knew she'd head to the city, though I didn't expect her to land in Austin."

He was silent then. Leah watched as he swallowed and put two fingers to his lips, perhaps to restrain a tear in his voice. Then he continued. "But I thought I would always have Logan. You know, parents aren't supposed to outlive their kids. He was my right arm. From the time he could walk, he was with me. I would take him out to the field with me and put him in the cab of the tractor. And he loved it. He always clamored to go with me. He wasn't just my son, the best one any dad could ask for; he was my little buddy and later on, he was my best friend."

His words stopped. Leah looked at her father-in-law and saw his small shoulders shake. Hands around his glass trembled.

She sat beside him and squeezed his arm again. Finally she whispered. "Logan adored you. He loved his mom, too, but you were especially close to him maybe because, as you said, you had been together so much. He was lucky to have you, and you were lucky to have him. No, you were both blest." Then she added, "So was I."

After a moment she slowly began again.

"You know, Merrill, do you think God gets mad at us if we love someone more than we love Him? I know we're supposed to love Him most, but that's just not logical. I loved Logan so much. I loved him more. Do you think He takes people away from us because we love them too much? None of this makes any sense to me. Then I wonder if there even is a God."

"I don't think it works like that. He's got to be bigger than that." Quietly he added, "He's bigger than that."

Changing the subject to a lighter vein, she observed, "By the way, I see my new friend has really taken to you, and from what I've noticed, he's pretty watchful of most men." As she spoke she watched Stranger lying at the feet of her father-in-law.

Merrill Cummings drank again from his ice tea and gently smiled. "We hit it off right away. I was out here one day last week, and he let me know we were going to be pretty good friends. He followed me down here, and we just sat and looked at the pond and some new ducks." He bent down and rubbed the big dog's ears. "I think you have a keeper, and I'm glad he's here with you."

Both the young woman and the older man sat in silence, each with their own memories of Logan and sipped their drinks.

"The yard looks nice. Did you have any trouble getting the little tractor started?" he asked finally.

"Started like a little trooper. And Stranger kept his eye on me the whole time. Even when he was lying under the lilac bush here, he had his chin on his front paws watching me. Guess he's going to be my caretaker," she concluded.

After several more minutes, darkness spread itself entirely across the pond and lay on the yard. Without the sun the night air became much cooler. Finally, the old man stood up and gave his empty glass to Leah.

"Just needed to sit a spell. I'm better now," he said.

"You can come in for a while if you like," she suggested.

"Thanks, but I'll just head home. Rachel'l be wondering where I am."

Stranger walked on the other side of Mr. Cummings as he and Leah walked up the hill to his car. At the car Leah kissed her father-in-law on the cheek and told him to bring Rachel and come back. She watched as he backed from the driveway. Then she addressed Stranger. "You like him a lot, too, don't you?"

Chapter Sixteen

Ladies Take Care of Ladies

Spring rolled into summer, and Leah began to emerge from beneath her umbrella of grief. Her garden flourished, and vegetables and fruits matured at a syncopated rate, which kept her busy during the evenings and weekends, canning and freezing and making jellies and jams.

Days at the clinic were no less busy. Even though her life had changed forever, business in the clinic continued on as before, with varying degrees of summer colds, ear infections and swimmers' ear, poison ivy allergies, and anything else that summer in the Midwest might offer.

One Friday afternoon at the end of July, Leah's open office door was filled with the presence of two of the doctors' nurses and the office receptionist. Leah looked up and quickly appraised them. She made a mental note that all three ladies were younger than she and then thought, *"Seems like everyone is anymore."*

Leah took stock of her three friends from the clinic.

Dana was a registered nurse who, like herself, had spent a few years after earning her degree, living and working in Des Moines. She, too, had returned to Glendale, proclaiming that guys in the capital were just too much into GQ, at least the ones who worked at the hospitals. And doctors were of another world.

She was attractive, but her personality often indicated an attitude of "Don't mess with me." The attitude that might have intimidated some men was the same attitude that served her well as a nurse in the clinic. Her directives to patients were received without rebuttal.

"Yes, you will make an appointment to have a colonoscopy ASAP." or "You're to take all 14 days of medicine. That's not 12, and that's not 13. I said 14."

She had many love interests, but, alas, few were long lasting. She wished for more.

Marcie was the youngster. She had gone to a small college in southern Iowa but had stopped at two years. She assisted the doctors and the nurses, but she wasn't certain medicine was where she belonged. Maybe in a few years she would go on to one of the state universities and look into a degree in business. On the other hand, if she met a nice young man who found the dish of matrimony to be appetizing, that would be alright, too. Her gentle personality allowed her to be led by Dana most of the time. And if Dana became so overpowering and tried to assume total control or, as Marcie put it, tried to "take prisoners" in their friendship, then she just stepped back. It was called self- preservation.

The third figure in the doorway was Polly. Divorced a year earlier, Polly was examining the world as a free soul. Her marriage had been one of a subtle bondage. Her husband, a lawyer, had been a dominant personality, and when Polly found that her identity was becoming a shadow of his, she had finally summoned enough courage to seek advice from another lawyer and, subsequently, to escape— from her husband and his command. She had chosen freedom over any kind of settlement. She laughingly said, "Give me liberty or give me death. Seems like I've heard that somewhere."

Behaving as the preordained speaker, Dana began. "It's Friday evening, and we're going over to Mission Falls to have a drink and get a bite to eat. They have a new restaurant, and we just wondered if you'd like to come along."

Marcie nodded assent and added, "Say you'll come and go with us. You haven't done anything for a long time, and it's not like we're going to steer you into trouble."

Leah looked at the three and was silent. To go out with "the girls" wasn't an invitation she thought at this point she really wanted to entertain.

Dana began again. "We usually get a bite to eat and maybe hit a movie if anything looks good. It's good to have you smiling and beginning to live again. Now let's put some meat back on those little bones of yours."

Marcie added, "You don't even have to go to the movie if you don't want. And maybe we won't find one anyway."

All this time Polly, the office's receptionist, had been silent. Polly was older than the other two and called herself "the senior citizen." Her divorce in some way allowed her to more easily identify with Leah's journey.

"You have to decide when you feel you're ready to start doing things again, but we just thought we'd let you know what we're doing tonight, and we'd enjoy having you along."

Leah turned her chair from her computer and faced the ladies.

"Do you go right after work? I had planned on freezing some corn this evening, but I guess I can do that tomorrow." She hesitated, giving vocal arguments to her decisions. "Okay, that might be fun. I think maybe I need to get out and do some of the girl stuff."

Three faces smiled, and Dana, apparently the voice of authority, said, "Good. I have to get out of these clothes, so I'll go home and shower and change." Then looking at her cohorts, she asked, "How about you two? Do you want to meet me back here at the clinic? And, Leah, you're just a mile or so off the highway, so we can swing by and pick you up. That all right with everyone?"

Leah smiled and thought, *"Why would you ever need a committee when you have Dana around?"* She agreed and thought to herself she might welcome a few minutes of escape at the farm first.

Later that afternoon as Leah drove into her drive way, Stranger appeared from the corner of the garage. With a touch to the door opener on her sun shield, she commanded the garage door to lift, and she drove into that shelter. She parked her car, assuming she would probably not be the driver tonight. Stranger stood at attention as she opened the door, giving her his most dedicated salute, the enthusiastic wagging of his tail.

"Hey, Buddy. If you're glad to see me, you can be assured I'm glad to see you. I swear, sometimes I really think you're smiling." She walked outside the garage and pressed the button to close the door. Kneeling down, she dropped her purse and lunch bag onto the ground and rubbed both hands in the fur of his neck. Then, for no reason that she knew, she began to cry. She dropped forward onto her knees and buried her face in his black and brown coat, both hands and arms embracing him. The tears turned into sobs until the sorrow had dissipated.

Finally, Leah sat up from Stranger. He looked at his friend with big brown/black eyes that were unblinking and watchful.

"Whew, don't know where that came from, Mr. Caretaker. Sometimes when I'm doing so well, " she mused aloud to him, "it's like I'm walking in the shallow end of the ocean, and a big, huge wave comes along and rolls me head over heels off my feet, and I come up gasping for air." She picked up her purse and bag and petted his head again.

"But, I'm so glad you were here to pull me out of the tide. That one was a tsunami."

Leah wiped her moist face with her hand and then bent down and brushed off her light beige trousers. "Guess it's a good thing I have a few minutes to refresh my eyes and comb my hair."

As she walked on into the house, Leah wondered if the emotional eruption had come about because she was making a step into a "girlfriends" social world. *Who would have ever thought a year ago that I would ever be here? Who asked for it?"* she thought.

Leah washed her face and reapplied mascara. She decided there wasn't a new restaurant in Mission Falls that warranted anything too dressy, so she stepped into newer jeans and tucked in a red shirt. Moccasins were comfortable, and as she was running a brush through her blonde hair, her doorbell rang.

She opened the door and smiled to see that Marcie was being greeted at the same time by Stranger. As large as he was, his wagging tail would have discredited any reason for her to fear him although Leah had been informed by delivery men that he was quite menacing when they made deliveries. He accepted most men only after they had been acknowledged by Leah. Ladies he viewed quite differently, and he had already checked Marcie out with his all-encompassing data collection of the canine sniff test. Leah noted Marcie was petting him between his ears.

"You ready for a wild women's night out?" Marcie grinned.

"You bet. And I'm getting a little hungry." Leah grabbed her purse and closed the door behind her. She looked at Stranger as he sat on the step, and said, "I'll be home in a couple of hours. Don't let anyone take anything."

Chapter Seventeen

Finding An Old Friend

The Mission Bells in Mission Falls had been a neighborhood bar with pool tables and dart games. The exterior had been revitalized with new red brick and a large mission bell enclosed in a stockade in front. Under new management and with a food license, new owners had envisioned a need for a quiet place for dining that would accommodate families with children on one side of the establishment and a bar and dance floor for young singles and couples on the other. If the band's music was good and was danceable and people wanted to linger on that side, they could elect to eat there as well. The quartet of ladies settled into a booth on the bar side and decided they would order cocktails or beer before they ordered dinner. After the four had studied the menu, the decision was made to remain in the bar for dinner.

The dining area made up half of the restaurant. The bar space was almost equal to the other half, and, therefore, provided enough room for a small local band and a dance floor. For the four ladies, conversation was an extension of events in the clinic and comments of the doctors' patients. All nurses had stories, usually humorous, of events that had occurred in the examining rooms.

"I took a phone call this afternoon from a female patient who was in yesterday. Dr. Green had ordered a suppository for her dad to take for his constipation, and she was asking, 'Since he has so much trouble swallowing pills, should I put it in his cereal?'" Marcie contributed.

Dana supplied a conversation with a single dad who had been given a prescription to fill for suppositories for his small constipated son. "He asked if he was supposed to take the aluminum foil off before he put it in his little boy's rectum."

The tales always brought laughter and were repeated many times when the nurses gathered. They usually ended their regalia with comments of "We should write a book…."

The small, local band set up and began to play hints of tunes, mostly country. Leah tried to listen to the conversations but was drawn to the music. At eight o'clock the leader of the small combo announced they would begin and that their music was to listen to or to dance to. Dana announced there were no new movies to be seen unless you were into another horror chamber story. *"Shudder,"* Leah shivered.

After some deliberation of the menu, Leah declared, "I eat so many sandwiches that I pack to the office, I don't know how many more tuna salads or PBJs I can eat. Then when I go home at night, I just don't cook. I mean, it's just me now. Sooooo, when I go out to eat, I have gotten into this thrifty, little habit of picking a pasta dish that I can take home for another meal. With the size of these side salads we're seeing tonight, I think I'll order spaghetti. I can probably get two more meals out of that."

"Sure," said Marcie. "And I guess that's why you're this size four figure. Me? I'll just eat the whole dinner. Maybe have dessert, too."

And with that, dinner choices were made. They remained in their booth, and Polly and Dana each ordered another beer. Marcie reconfirmed her role as the designated driver and joined Leah with a cup of coffee. They sat with their Styrofoam containers of leftovers and occasionally actually listened to a country tune.

Leah sat next to the wall in the booth and listened, sometimes to conversation, sometimes to the halting, unsteady beat of the amateur music. Playing with the handle of her coffee cup, she was vaguely aware that she was being watched. She turned her head towards the bar and saw a familiar face, a face that had always belonged to Mission Falls. She blinked and smiled as Ryan James mouthed to her, "Leah?"

She shyly waved and said in return, "Ryan? Ryan James?"

Ryan studied the group for a moment, and after deciding it was safe to venture into unknown waters, turned from the group of men who held his attention and walked the few steps to the booth of Leah and her friends. His presence at the end of their table demanded that all the ladies stop their conversation and look up.

Dana was the first to speak. "Ryan. How have you been? We're having a ladies night out."

Ryan turned his gaze from Leah and looked directly at Dana. "Well, I'm fine, thank you." He looked at the other two ladies in the booth. Sticking his hand out to Polly and Marcie, he introduced himself. "I'm Ryan James. I knew our new Mission Bells would be good for our town, and this just validates how right I was." Looking at Leah, then, he smiled, "I'm glad it brought out an old friend."

Dana watched, noticing the attention he was giving to her office manager. Looking at her friends, she commented, "I noticed you talking to your buddies there a while ago when we were eating. Do you come here every Friday night?"

"Well, this is only the third week it's been in business, but, yes, I was here when it opened at the beginning of the month, and I guess I was here last weekend, too," he concluded. "Obviously, it's going to be good for Missions Falls, as I'm witnessing right now."

Leah was listening and observing the behaviors of her friends as she leaned against the back of the booth. She watched as Ryan smoosed the ladies. As she remembered from years ago, he portrayed self-confidence and ease when he talked. She was always impressed with his eyes fringed by long, long lashes. Nothing had changed about them, except for the addition of a few slight wrinkles at the corners. With a black Stetson sitting squarely on top of his head, she noticed slight graying at the temples. *"Not fair,"* she mused. *"Women get gray haired, and they look older. Men? They just look distinguished."*

She watched her friends' responses to Ryan's charm. Polly, like herself, was quiet and appeared watchful.

Marcie was enjoying the attentions of an older gentleman, but Dana was most receptive. In fact, Leah sensed a connection between those two that might have been present before tonight.

On the other side of the booth, Dana nudged Polly to scoot down, and she, too, slid further along the seat. Dana patted the end of the bench and said to Ryan, "Here, have a seat a minute."

Ryan glanced at Leah and then seated himself beside Dana. Looking across the table, he asked, "How are you doing? It's good to see you out."

"I'm doing a whole lot better. My friends here asked me to join them this evening, so this is something a little new to me." Leah spoke slowly, considering her words carefully. "We've had a fun evening, and the food's been good. I think I'm playing a whole new ball game. Guess I'll have to learn the rules. Thank goodness for friends, though." She looked at him, and asked, "How have you been? What are you doing now?"

Ryan scratched at the label of his bottle of beer and looked at her. "Well, after college at Arizona, I came back to Iowa and went to Iowa State. Now I'm a doctor." He paused and grinned, "But I care for animals. I'm a veterinarian."

"Now why does that not surprise me? Of course. You'd make a great vet."

Bringing the conversation back to herself, Dana asked, "Do you dance? This group isn't too bad. I mean, they actually have a beat."

Leah mused, *"You really have to listen to hear a constant beat, but, oh, well. Music is in the ear of the beholder."*

Ryan scooted his empty Bud bottle to the center of the table and stood. "I think I can stumble around a little. Come on. We'll see what we can do."

Dana slid out of the booth and walked in front of him to the dance floor. Leah leaned back again and looked at her empty coffee cup. She wondered if this evening would be more than just dinner. Did all of this define a 'girls' night out'? She felt a pang of guilt again in leaving her comfort zone of Friday night at home...alone and with Stranger.

Chapter Eighteen

A Walk With Stranger

Leah opened her eyes to bright sunlight which had drifted in and was waiting silently in her bedroom. Pushing the pillow into a larger mound beneath her head, she was able to see the numbers on her clock. 7:27. Late. She lazily dropped her arm over the side of the bed and let her fingers play in the coat of the large dog lying on the floor there. That produced a happy reaction...a thumping of his tail.

"You did let me sleep this morning, didn't you, Little Boy? It's going on7:30." She rolled back into the middle of the bed, remembering the night before.

The evening with her three friends had been pleasant, but she questioned again this morning if she was ready to go out. It didn't feel quite right. Logan had been gone not quite a full year yet. She had not taken many nights out with girlfriends when he was alive. She didn't have a need or great desire for company with girlfriends. Besides being her husband and lover, Logan was her best friend. She enjoyed time spent with him and preferred his company to most others. That wasn't to say she didn't appreciate time and small talk with girlfriends, but their presence wasn't a commodity she sought.

Last night had been enjoyable, and seeing Ryan James again had been a pleasant surprise. He was certainly as handsome as he had been twenty some years ago when they attended high school, albeit from rival schools.

Ryan with the beautiful eyes. Not much had changed in his appearance. Tall, dark hair, engaging smile, and a manner that made you feel you were the only person he wanted to talk with. Dana and he had danced a couple of tunes the band had played. Then when they had returned to their booth, one of the men with whom Ryan had been talking came over and had asked Marcie to dance. Ryan had sat down in the booth beside Leah. After talking with both her and Dana, he asked Leah to dance. Leah had felt very uncomfortable with that. She remembered a time when she had loved to dance, but Logan always said he didn't have any rhythm. Therefore, they hadn't danced much. She had apologized to Ryan but declined. He danced then with Polly and again with Dana, as did his friend.

When the band quit for a second break, Leah suggested, "Anyone for heading back East? It's way past this woman's bedtime." She had a feeling that Dana and Marcie might have stayed longer.

Now in the morning, lying on her back in bed and watching the rotating blades of the ceiling fan, she was leisurely pulling to the front of her mind the pictures from the previous night. The July night had not cooled much, and the central air was welcome. Finally, she began serious motions to begin the day. As was the usual practice now, she laid her bare feet lightly in Stranger's hair and slowly moved them back and forth along his back and side. The tail slapped against the floor, and then he was up.

Leah pulled on cut-off jean shorts and a cotton tee. Tomatoes and peppers were waiting to be made into salsa. She tried to dismiss the events of the previous evening so that she could dismiss the guilt she'd felt in being out without Logan. Way down in some tucked away crevasse of her mind, she held an accusatory feeling she had cheated on him. The top part of her mind, the part right behind her forehead, did not acknowledge that, but the feeling, even as a gray shadow, lingered there.

Leah felt her chest tighten. She busied herself brushing her teeth, wishing she could brush away the sadness that crept into her bed with her so often at night and stayed with her as she arose. She was glad to see sunshine. Unspeakably good medicine.

Stranger was ushered outdoors where he proceeded to make his security check of the yard and barn lot. Leah busied herself with the promised salsa and juice. Healing occurs hardly noticed as minutes and hours are filled by busy-ness. By evening Leah felt good about a Saturday alone. She had prepared food, tidied her house, and finished laundry. As evening became apparent, she stepped onto her porch and felt a break in the heat of the July day. The air had picked up a soft breeze from the south, making the leaves in the tops of the trees dance to their own music.

"Might be a good evening for a walk with my buddy," she said aloud. "We haven't walked up into the woods lately." She changed from her sandals to worn tennis shoes and stepped out onto the back step. Stranger was ready. Of course. Checking his water pan, she added more from the hose, and turning to him said, "Ready for a walk, Stranger? I think you're getting lazy."

They walked down the sloping yard, past the gazebo with the shady lilac bush and past the pond. They walked across a ravine at the far end of the yard and along the trail into the woods. Only a couple of acres had been allowed to remain uncultivated. Logan and she had enjoyed walking in these few acres in the spring when he had a few hours free from planting crops, in the summer on evenings such as this, and in the fall as the colors of oranges, greens and golds were their most magnificent. And, of course, winter provided a totally different scape.

This day as they walked, Stranger explored ahead of her, running back from time to time to check on her. Earlier in the spring, she had searched along the ravine and at the base of mostly dying elms for mushrooms. Logan could spot the morels long before she found them, and she had been known to stand in a patch of them before she realized they were even near, much to the enjoyment of Logan, of course. She accused him of being able to smell them. *"May be,"* she still thought.

She picked up a sturdy stick and proceeded to use it as a walking cane. Stranger had made a return trip and was walking at her side. Suddenly he stopped abruptly, in front of her now, nearly causing her to stumble. He stood perfectly still. Ears back and legs locked. She had seldom heard him growl, but from deep in his chest came a deep rumbling. The hair at his shoulders and neck stood as a threatening "Grrrrrwwwlll" came from deep in his throat.

He stood squarely in front of her now, and if she had wanted to move on, she would have had to step over him.

She looked in the direction he was staring. On a slope away from the trees, sunning himself in the late afternoon sunshine was an animal she had never seen before. The gray and black, long-nosed animal had spread itself flat in the dirt. Now as it sensed their presence, it stood. It turned to fiercely face them, and Leah recognized the striped face as a badger. *"We don't have badgers in Iowa. Not that I know of,"* she thought.

The animal was not advancing towards them, but it wasn't backing away, either. "Come on, Stranger. Now's not the time to show me how brave you are. I really don't want to know." She heard her voice pleading, "You don't want to start anything with him. He's a mean, mean fighting machine. Let's just back away."

She began a slow retreat while Stranger stood. The badger remained quiet on the side of the hill. Leah was aware of her heart ka-thudding in her chest. She had never seen a badger on this farm, or for that matter, anywhere in Iowa. She had never felt any sense of danger on this farm. She wondered if Stranger had not stopped her, would she have walked up and on it. She knew that badgers were fierce fighters and weren't usually the aggressor, but they weren't likely to turn and run if they felt they were being cornered.

"Let's just say we'll let him have this corner of the property," she said quietly to Stranger as he trotted up to her. "That's his land, and we'll not bother him. And that means you don't go looking for him someday when I'm not around."

The two walked on in silence, but she did make a definite effort to rub his head. Then she said, "Sometimes I think you take care of me as well as Logan did."

Chapter Nineteen

Baby Sitting J. R.

July limped out, dragging and sweating from the summer heat. Leah's lawn mowing declined to one Saturday morning every two weeks and quite often to three. She watered her small garden of flowers and a few vegetables, but rural water was never as nourishing as rain water. The plants continued to live but were not as productive as they were when the summer wasn't as hot or as dry.

Dana and Marcie had asked the next Friday after they had driven to Mission Falls to go out with them again. That had been the Friday evening Leah had volunteered to baby-sit her new five month old nephew, John Richard Weeks.

"Please don't forget me," she said. "I do want to go with you again, but I told Paul and Emily I would watch J.R. so they could have a date. A quiet, much-needed date." She still had reservations about going out 'without Logan'. She still harbored mixed feelings of some pleasure and some guilt in going out, but she was trying to deal with that. She had to recognize and then address the guilt issue. But, besides that, she did want to spend time with her new nephew.

Leah had been home about a half hour when her doorbell rang. Before she could answer the summons, Stranger had greeted her brother and Emily with their prized bundle.

"Oh, I've been looking forward to this," Leah exclaimed. Taking the portable car seat from her brother, she set the small chair on her living room carpet, unsnapped the restraining belt, and picked up the blond haired charmer. "I haven't seen you since our Fourth of July picnic, and, look at you. You've grown a yard. And you're a little chunk." She held him to her shoulder as he looked at his new surroundings and back at Leah.

Paul settled onto the floor a bag filled with diapers, baby formula, jars of baby food, and a few squeaky, chewable toys. Emily followed behind with a collapsible play pen.

She laughed, "See how much I get to carry him? When Paul's around I have to race him to get a turn. So here we are, Paul with baby and me with Pack N Play."

Emily accompanied her complaint with a wink in Leah's direction. In just a minute, she deployed the portable bed.

Directions were given regarding expected time of the next feeding and how to treat a gassy tummy which occurred if he drank too fast from his bottle. The couple left with reassurance they would call between dinner and the movie and would come home if she needed them.

Leah had planned on doing nothing except hold J.R. and play with him. After spreading a soft blanket on the carpet, she placed him on his tummy. She lay on the floor beside him and was amused to see Stranger wag his tail and crawl closer to the blanket. As the baby made attempts to roll over and creep, Stranger appeared to be perplexed. His gaze was on J.R. but with occasional looks to Leah. She laughed at his concern and said, "Does this little boy bother you? Not to worry, Stranger. He's okay."

Eventually, J.R. did fuss and noting the time, Leah surmised he was probably hungry. She opened a jar of mixed vegetables and then a jar of pureed bananas. J.R. finished all that with formula. She rocked him and waited for the obligatory, and in this case, monster burp. Just as the phone rang with questions from Paul, she was aware of a need to change the baby's diaper.

In anticipation of her first assignment to baby-sit, Leah had bought the first book of a promising library that she could read to him and to any other of his siblings or cousins who might arrive in the future. They settled back in the rocking recliner, and she read. One book. Two books. Three books. Four books. But they were small books. He lay back in her arms and slept. Leah looked down. At the side of her chair lay the German shepherd baby sitter. He was stretched out, apparently listening to the stories if for no other reason than to hear the melody of Leah's voice. After some minutes of snuggling with her sleeping nephew, Leah placed him undisturbed in the Pack 'n Play.

Friday night. She stepped outdoors to water her garden. Returning to the kitchen, she placed a bag of popcorn in the microwave. Then she peered into the living room to check on J.R. The small child with the rolls of baby fat on his little legs was sleeping peacefully. Sleeping beside his portable bed was his new four-legged friend.

Leah smiled and was aware of a great sense of peace. She thought, *"At least for the moment, I just can't think of a better way to spend a Friday evening."*

Chapter Twenty

Annie's Baby

Paul and Emily retrieved their offspring before midnight. They had driven to Mission Falls to check out the Mission Bells and had found a movie they thought they wanted to see. They discovered old friends and, consequently, revisited the bar side of the new restaurant where they enjoyed an evening drink and conversation that included more than baby stories. The movie was put on hold until they had another evening out, hopefully. J.R. slept peacefully when he was retrieved and didn't awaken even while being strapped into his baby car seat.

Leah prepared to close and lock the front door but was aware that Stranger apparently wanted to go outdoors. "I thought you did your nightly duty earlier," she remarked to him. "Do you prefer being outdoors tonight? Can't blame you a whole lot. You just like the night air better than the air conditioning, don't you?"

She opened the door again, and giving her a look which seemed to question his own actions, Stranger walked out the open door and stood on the front step. He looked back at her again and then walked off the stoop.

Leah stood at the door and watched as he ambled around the side of the house. He was headed to the barn and the cattle lot, which surprised her. She thought he would sleep in the gazebo.

Turning off the lights of the kitchen and the den, Leah walked into the bedroom. She had remarked to Stranger that she would leave on the air, but after noting the breeze when letting him out, she decided to turn it off and opened the windows instead. She turned on the ceiling fan and readied for bed.

The smile she felt on her lips remembering the sweetness of the baby was followed by a deep sadness at the fact she and Logan had never had a chance to share such an experience. Sleep, a pattern which was gradually weaving itself back into her life, came soon after.

Shortly before three that morning, Leah was wakened by Stranger's frantic barking beneath her bedroom window. *"Coon? Deer?"* she asked herself. *"He doesn't usually bark unless someone's in the drive."*

She stepped between the blowing sheers at the open window. "Stranger, what are you barking at?" She looked out but saw nothing amiss. Stranger was barking and running back and forth. She walked to the back door and turned on the porch light.

"Stranger, what's going on?" she asked again. Her four legged companion was running toward the barn lot. He stopped and looked back at her, then returned to her, still barking. "Just a minute so I can put something on my feet. I'll be there. What are you so upset about?"

Leah stuck her feet into the worn sandals by the door and followed. Stranger ran to the barn and crawled through the doggie door which Merrill Cummings had made years earlier for the family's outside pets. Leah opened the half door to the barn and turned on a light switch.

The dog ran quickly to Annie, who was on the floor of the stall where Simon had led her the evening before. He had remarked that Annie would soon be having her calf, and it might be a good idea to put her in the barn by herself.

Although most cows have their calves without assistance, some have trouble, especially first time mothers. Leah ran to Annie, who was struggling with pain at each contraction. Obviously, labor had begun several hours before, but she was not able to birth her baby.

"Oh, my little Annie. I don't know what to do for you," she cried. "If Logan were here, he could pull your baby out, but I don't know how to even begin. Sweetie, I'll get some help."

She ran back to the house and called Merrill. After informing him of Annie's situation, she asked frantically, "Merrill, what should I do? What would Logan have done? I'd call a vet, but I don't know who he would have called since Doc Cooper retired. What should I do?"

The elder Mr. Cummings had been brought to a full awakening when he heard Leah's voice on the phone.

"No one's come into Glendale to take his place yet. Give Doc James in Mission Falls a call. Don't know if he has an answering service to handle an emergency or not. He'll be in the phone book. I'll get dressed and be right over." Reassuringly, he added, "Don't worry, Honey. Annie's going to be alright."

Leah found Dr. Ryan James' number in the directory. "Phone answered day or night," his ad said in the yellow pages. She called the number listed for emergencies. The answering service picked up.

"Can you call a message into Dr. James? This is Leah Cummings in Glendale. My young cow is having a birthing problem"

Leah tried to keep her voice steady. *"After all. This is just an animal. Merrill will be here, and I know she'll be alright. I mean, he's seen these things all the time, hasn't he? In fact, he could probably pull the calf by himself."*

Aloud she added, "If you would just have him call me back. Please!" Leah provided her phone number and the night service agent assured her she would call the doctor as soon as she hung up.

"He's always very prompt about getting right back to his patients."

Sitting on a stool at the kitchen bar, she put the phone back onto its cradle and waited. What felt like hours was actually nine minutes.

"Leah, this is Ryan James," the voice said. "My answering service called and said you have a cow in trouble? Can you tell me how far along she is?"

The calm and deliberateness of his voice reassured Leah. "I wish I had paid more attention to this stuff when Logan was alive," she replied. "I can't tell you much.

Stranger woke me with his barking, and she's thrashing around quite a bit, and it looked like the calf's hooves were protruding. I guess I wouldn't be so frantic if this little mama wasn't a favorite of mine. Almost a pet. No, she IS a pet."

Ryan's voice was comforting and sounded knowledgeable. "Let me get dressed, and I'll be over. I think I know where you live, but give me exact directions. Hate pulling into the wrong farmer's driveway at 3:30 in the morning."

Directions were given. Shortly after she hung up, she heard the sound of a car in the driveway.

"Dad must have moved faster than he has in years to get here this fast," she mused. She ran quickly into her bedroom and changed into her farming clothes of cut-offs and tee. Then she ran out the back door and caught up with Merrill on his way to the barn.

"Did you get a'hold of Dr. James?" he asked, as he scurried to the barn.

"Yes, and he said he'd be right over. I hope he hurries."

"If Logan were here, he'd help me pull the calf. I use to pull them out, but sometimes you lose the calf as well as its mother," he reminisced.

As they stood watching Annie, Leah softly began to cry. "I don't want to lose her, too. I mean, it's just a little cow, but I certainly don't want to lose my little Annie."

The old man put his arm lightly across her shoulders. "Doc'll be here soon, and she's going to be okay. She's not the first little heifer this has happened to."

In the time he had allotted, Dr. James drove into the drive to the farm lot and strode into the barn. Over summer shorts and an Iowa State tee, he wore orange coveralls, dressed for such a chore as pulling a calf from the uterus of its mother. Glancing at Leah and her father-in-law, he said, "So the little one decided he'd make things difficult for his mom, huh?" He walked over to the struggling Annie and studied the situation.

Watching him in action, Leah was impressed at his preciseness. He took measurements, temperature…

*   *   *   *   *   *   *

The pot of coffee had perked when the two men walked back to the house less than an hour later, accompanied by Stranger. Ryan removed his coveralls at the door, then strode confidently into the kitchen.

He looked at Leah and announced, "Well, Grandma, you have a grandson. Mother and baby are doing well, but they're both pretty tired. I'll give you some antibiotic medicine for your cow to ward off any infection, and there's some supplement for the calf. You can just put the medicine in the little lady's feed for a day or two, and I think Mr. Cummings here can help you get some serum down the little bull's throat."

He washed his hands at the sink, and looking at Merrill as Leah filled three mugs of coffee, he said, "If you see any signs of any infection or if you witness any strange behavior, like if they don't bounce back in a day or two, give me a call." He seated himself on a stool at the bar.

Merrill said, "I doubt if I'm going back to bed at this hour, so I might as well have the coffee. Got any bread for Texas toast and any more of that wild plum and peach jam?" he asked, "Might as well plod on into the day since it's already begun." He seated himself on the stool next to Dr. James.

At five in the morning in July the sun was making its appearance. Leah listened as the two learned men talked about whatever men from the plains talk about at five in the morning or any other time of the day…weather, crops, market prices, and if it was their passion…politics. At five in the morning, Leah fried bacon, eggs, and frozen hash browns. She found bread for Texas toast and routed out some homemade jam.

Reluctantly, and as if watching out for Leah's well-being, her father-in-law finally finished an early breakfast, shared enough of his opinions and decided to leave for the morning. Ryan walked out with him but said he would make one more spot check of Annie and her new son before he left. He returned to find Leah waiting at the back stoop. The sun was wearing its finest apparel and was assuring all who were awake at that hour that it would be a beautiful Iowa morning.

"Ryan, tell me how much I owe you, and I'll pay you before you leave." She held up her check book and pen.

Ryan smiled and said, "I've been thinking about that. Usually getting a man out of bed at three in the morning, driving twenty some miles to be met by a woman whose hair's not been combed, and then pulling her cow's calf would run into, oh, maybe, hundreds and hundreds of dollars, but like I said, I've been giving it some thought just now, and I'm thinking maybe I should just forgive the charge if she'd consider going to the State Fair with me in a couple of weeks in Des Moines."

Leah watched as the familiar grin spread across his face. *"I'm pretty sure this sounds like I'm being asked for a date,"* she thought. *"It's been such a long time, I mean a long, long time."*

Aloud she said, "Ryan, I'm not sure I'm ready to do that. Part of me says that would be the best way to spend a day, and another part of me says, "No, you can't go.""

Ryan looked steadily at her. "I don't mean to rush you, but why don't you listen to the part that's telling you it would be a great way to spend the day? If you wanted to drive to my house, since it's on the way to Des Moines, we'd just leave your car, and drive up there for the day. Just one day of corn dogs, fresh lemonade, and anything you want to see or do."

Leah didn't speak. Then quietly she replied, "I guess I can do that. Maybe this would give me a chance to go up on Friday night and spend the night with Chris Use-To-Be-Jordan, my old college roommate. Then you could pick me up there, or I could meet you at the fairgrounds."

Ryan smiled, "That'll work. I'll call you and get Chris's address and phone number."

Leah felt they had arrived at a fair compromise. It was a step out and, hopefully, a step forward. "I got off pretty easy, didn't I?" she asked. "I really, really, really appreciate you and what you did tonight. Thank you."

She looked at Stranger who appeared to be listening to the conversation. "This all okay with you, Buddy?" Stranger looked at her and wagged his tail as if in approval.

Ryan walked to his pick-up, and Leah turned to walk into the kitchen. Then she knelt down and ran both hands through Stranger's hair. "And I really, really, really appreciate you, my good man."

Chapter Twenty One

First Date…Again

The Iowa State Fair began in the middle of the second week of August. Ryan had called at the beginning of the week after Annie's baby, Abner, was born on the pretense of inquiring how the two patients were doing. After discussing the progress of the two animals, Ryan arrived at the real reason for the call.

"Well, Abner's grandma, I've been thinking about this visit to the state fair, and I thought you might prefer to attend the first Saturday. That way, you wouldn't miss any work or have to take a day's vacation. I have to admit, that would be a good day for me to be gone. Besides, I have it in my mind that might be a special day for entertainment," he explained.

"I think that might be the best day, too. So often if you go the second Saturday, vendors and exhibitors are already taking some of their exhibits and crafts home. Some of the livestock is gone, too. And I'm sure that's what would pique your interest." She took a breath and continued. "It will definitely be one of the busiest days, but

I agree the first Saturday would be best. Now, cross your fingers it's not a hundred degrees. In the shade, I might add."

Ryan was in agreement so arrangements were made to meet at the State Capitol where both would park their cars and ride the shuttle to the fairgrounds.

Leah left work early that Friday, and Stranger met her at the garage. It appeared he either waited for her return from work each afternoon at the door of the garage or he was acutely aware of her car as it approached on the gravel road. Never mind. He was always patiently waiting. Leah didn't drive into the garage but parked in the driveway. Stranger followed her into the house, sensing there was or would be a change in their Friday night routine. He lagged behind as she walked into the bedroom and watched as she folded clothes she would be wearing and placed them in a traveling bag. Weather reports had promised the Saturday would be warm. *"Not hot,"* she hoped. *"Just warm."* But August in Iowa was usually hot. She dared to hope for a break in the heat. She packed light jeans, as well as walking shorts. No cut-offs, and she felt she was way too old for shorter shorts. She added a couple of tee-tops, a short sleeved shirt, another pair of sandals, and pajamas for her overnight stay.

Stranger lay on the floor at the foot of her bed and watched.

Then Leah addressed an issue she'd never considered before. Since Logan's death, she had not removed her wedding rings. There had been no reason. She was still married. Now she was distressed. She walked into the den and sat on the sofa, the same sofa where Logan had held her and had been so upset after the car accident.

"You promised you would be around to take care of me," she cried. "You promised. I don't know if I'm ready for this. I don't think I can do it." She twisted the rings on the third finger of her left hand. "I can't wear them when I'm with another man, though. That's not fair to him. It'll look like he's with a married woman, and, for that matter, I won't be looking so good either."

Leaning back in the sofa and with tears on her cheeks, Leah pulled at the rings. Stranger sat in the doorway and studied her behavior. She pushed the rings back onto her finger and rose from the couch. "I can't do this," she concluded.

She walked to the walled book shelves and picked up the photo of her and Logan, the photo that had been taken for the church directory, the church they only occasionally had attended. The photographer had asked that Logan put his arm around her waist, to which Logan had teased, "Aw, do I have to?" She had smacked him on the arm, and he had groaned in mock pain. Then there was the wedding photo, and on the shelf second from the top was the photo of him in his Marine Dress Blues. She wept silently, and then walked over to Stranger, who had moved to the floor in the center of the room. Sitting down in front of him, she crossed her legs and leaned forward, touching her chin to the top of his head. He lay still as he felt her tears and listened to her quietly crying. Finally she sat up and said, "If I'm to get on with this life, I guess I need to take them off, don't I? What do you think? Should I leave them home?"

Stranger lifted his head, and, looking at her, thumped his tail on the carpet.

"I guess that's as much of an 'okay' as I'm going to get from you, isn't it? But that'll do." She scratched his head, brought her fingers down, and very gently scratched his face under his eyes and along his long nose. "Thank you, my dear friend."

Leah had heard the doctors in her clinic advise their patients of an old remedy handed down eons ago from their ancestors and had never been disproved. When a physical wound is open and raw, wash or soak the wound with warm salt water. Leah made an observation of a comparable basis. "When the soul is wounded and open and raw, let the warm salt water from your tears bring its healing." The tears came less and less often now, and the soul was healing.

She finished packing after removing her rings and setting them in her jewelry box. She set out enough dry dog food for Stranger in his bowl in a corner of the deck and filled his water dish. He followed her to the car, looking sad as she stowed her bag in the trunk. Opening the door, she turned and reminded him of his responsibilities. "Don't leave the place, and make sure you guard everything. And look in on Annie and Abner. I'll be home tomorrow night." She affectionately petted him goodbye.

*   *   *   *   *   *   *

It was good to see Chris and her husband. He was still a UPS driver and had found that to be the perfect vocation which gave him the time he wanted to still be part of a locally known band. They had a son and a daughter. Chris remarked, "There aren't any more genders, so since we had one of each, we decided to stop." Conversation covered the events of the last year since Logan's death, but Leah had already learned that for those people who hadn't gone through the loss of a spouse, her sorrow would be heard but not even remotely felt, and she understood that. That's just the way it was. At the same time she knew she could never have any understanding of the loss of a child, except she knew it had to be horrible.

As planned, she met Ryan at a designated spot where parking was allowed on the grounds of the Iowa Capitol the next morning. Even at ten a.m. parking spots were filling. She was lucky to find one near their meeting place, and that was only by chance as a young couple was backing out of their place and leaving As she approached the bench, she saw Ryan already seated and talking on a cell phone. She waved and walked more quickly.

"Have you been here long?" she asked. "I thought I was making pretty good time."

Closing the lid on his phone, he grinned and teased, "It feels like forever."

"Smarty." Then she asked, "Do you have a patient who needs you? As in pulling a new calf?"

"I was just picking up my messages, but there was only one. Looks like everyone's giving their vet a day off.

Actually, I do have quite a competent staff and a bright young intern who's been helping me."

He had stood to greet her, but since others were standing in small groups to the side of the bus stop, they both had a seat again on the bench. The wait was short, and Ryan gave the bus driver the four required quarters. They found a seat at the back of the long vehicle.

"It's been such a long time since I rode one of these from West Des Moines. Chris worked downtown. I didn't, but when I rode the bus down town to hit some of the high spots on Fridays nights with her for whatever reason, I never stopped thinking it was fun." She looked at him and asked, "What time did you get to the big city?"

Stretching his long legs as far in front of him as he could in the confined space, he said, "Actually, I drove up last night. I met a friend of mine who finished grad school with me at Iowa State. He went into veterinary college, too, but he stayed here in the Des Moines area so I bunked last night with him and his wife….in his new five bedroom house." He looked at Leah and added, "I wasn't sure you'd enjoy looking at all of the livestock and machinery. Well, really, I didn't cover all the machinery, either. But, if I were to tell you the whole truth….I felt it was sort of my duty to check out all the corn dogs and lemonade stands before you got here."

"And did you get them all checked out?"

"Uh huh. Oh, and by the way, they're featuring deep fried Twinkies this year." He grinned. "There's only so much I'll do for you, so you're on your own on that one, Miss Leah."

"Dang. So goes chivalry out the door. Already."

The shuttle ride to the fairgrounds was a ten minute trip, and Leah was feeling relieved about the morning. She ducked her head and from the corners of her eyes, she studied her date. Not much was different from the man she had met at the Mission Bells when he wore his black cowboy hat nor different from the man in his orange coveralls, his uniform for delivering wedged calves. Today he wore chino shorts, an Iowa State tee shirt, and sandals. Rather generic, but he definitely passed muster. He was not one who had added a tummy, as Logan hadn't either.

A short walk onto the Grand Concourse, and she asked, "Well, where do you suppose we'll find the best lemonade?"

"I'm so glad you asked because I was feeling a little gaunt myself. Lack of sugar, you know. What's it been since we got here? Ten minutes?" He squeezed the back of her neck with a large, calloused hand and said, "Good thing I'm prepared. Best lemonade's just around this corner."

Leah realized how much she had to look up to him. If he were nearly six feet tall in high school, then he must be a few inches over six feet now. And she hadn't grown even half an inch over her five feet.

The day was all she could have hoped for and more. The sun didn't try to outdo itself with its heat, and the light Iowa breezes were cooling. Ryan was a good sport and walked with her through the various buildings, all exhibiting the finer points of life on the rural scene, introduction of items from a metropolitan world and items from the classic country venue. They enjoyed the free shows of entertainment, many featuring their college era headliners performing on stages scattered throughout the grounds.

Mid-afternoon, they sat in the shade at a picnic table and Leah asked, "Ryan, did you ever marry? Or is this the part where you say, 'Guess that's none of your business?'"

Ryan turned the cup of his new drink, sweet iced tea, and replied, "Not a secret. No, I never married. I was engaged to a vet student from Philadelphia, but she decided she didn't want any part of rural Iowa, and I was equally sure I didn't want any part of the eastern scene. She wanted to return to her home and play doctor to small animals in her family's up-scale neighborhood. I was sorry when it was over, but it wasn't going to work out, and I've not found anyone who's been a match since."

Leah persisted with questions. "Have you not dated others since you started your practice? When we were in Mission Falls a couple of weeks ago, I wondered if you might have had something going with Dana at some time. She seemed to be very interested, and if there's anything going on, I don't want to be part of that picture.

"Nope. There's nothing there. We went out a couple of times, but Dana has a personality that doesn't jive with mine. I would have a hard time taking orders, and I'm pretty sure that would be a requirement if you were to be with her as a couple. We had fun, but we talked about it on our last date, and I told her I just didn't want to take matters of the relationship any further. She pretty much agreed. I was glad to see her in the restaurant, and I'm glad we had a chance to talk. And we did when we danced. She's a good egg, and she'll make a good match for someone who needs to be told what to do. Yep, that'll be a good pairing."

He paused and sipped his drink. Changing the subject, he said, "I was sorry to hear about Logan. There wasn't one person who could have said anything bad about him."

"Thank you. I appreciate that. There was a time I thought I couldn't breathe again, but life is beginning to feel good again, and I know he'd want me to go on. I never in a thousand years dreamt I'd be here without him."

Both Leah and Ryan were quiet, reflecting on the words they had shared. Finally Leah spoke, "I've thought about the difference of losing someone through death and losing someone you love who walks away. I feel like when a person just walks away from a relationship and from someone who still loves him or her, that person leaves and takes his love with him. But when someone dies, you know you will never ever see him again, but like when Logan died, he left his love behind. It'll always be here with me." As she finished her soliloquy, she felt the tears inching into the corners of her eyes.

"You know a couple of years ago, after we'd had a pretty good snowfall and it was darned cold, I had to go to a funeral visitation after work. One of our favorite patients had passed away, and several of us girls from the office wanted to attend the visitation. Anyway, when I slid out of the front seat of the car, I must have pushed my leather gloves out onto the street. I didn't realize it until I made it home. When I walked into the kitchen, Logan asked why I looked so glum. I told him I had lost the leather gloves he had given me for Valentine's Day, the first Valentine's Day we had gone together. He told me not to fuss over it, and the next evening when I came home from work, he met me at the kitchen door and asked what I would give him if he had found my black gloves. I told him I would give him the world's biggest kiss. With that, he pulled my stiff, wrinkled leather gloves from behind his back and presented them to me. Would you believe he had gone back to the area where I had parked my car on the street and then had walked up and down the street until he found my gloves in the freezing slush? The city maintainer had bladed them up against the curb. Can you believe that? Was that not above and beyond the call of duty?"

Ryan slipped his hand across the table and squeezed her fingers. "Leah, he didn't want to leave you, not you. He was a lucky guy....and I think you were a lucky lady."

The afternoon slipped away quickly. They had taken another break in their exploring when Ryan said, "I took the liberty of buying two tickets to tonight's performance. Since I donate to the Fair fundraisers, I get early notices of booked entertainers, and I can buy advance tickets. When I saw who was performing tonight, I went ahead and ordered two tickets. At the time I didn't even know for sure I was coming today or not. I thought if I wasn't I'd give them to my receptionist and her fiancé," He looked at the ends of his dusty toes inside his dusty sandals and said no more.

Finally Leah asked, "Well, who's playing tonight?"

"Aw, I don't even know if you'd be interested."

"Oh, come on. And I'm not going to beg you."

"I ordered tickets to see George Strait," he responded slowly.

"You did not!" Leah squealed. "I adore him. Well, his music. No, him. And you really do have tickets to see him tonight?"

Ryan took his time and finally responded, "Yup. Third row. Pretty much in the center."

"No way! I thought we'd be on the road home before it was too dark, but there's no way I'm leaving now, even if I have to take you down and wrestle the tickets out of your billfold," she threatened. "Why didn't you tell me this earlier?"

He grinned even broader. "Let's get back to that part about you wrestling me for the tickets. I use to know a few moves, but I could probably be pinned. Dang, that sounds like fun."

"Oh, shut up," she laughed. "Now why didn't you tell me earlier?"

Half seriously, Ryan explained that he wanted to take her to the State Fair, but he didn't want her to say yes just so she could see George Strait."

"Oh, not counting the fact that you said you were forgiving my vet bill?" she queried.

"I suppose that might have been a bit of a carrot, wasn't it?"

"Maybe it was, but honestly, Ryan, this has been a great day. And a chance to see George Strait is just frosting on the cake."

They ate steaks at the Cattlemen's Barn, sipped a beer in the Budweiser tent, and finished the evening listening to the music of George Strait and his Ace in the Hole Band.

Finally, the shuttle took them back to their cars on the Capitol lawn.

"Ryan, I feel like I've taken a big step forward today. I mean I've had a wonderful day, and I ventured out of my box, my box of grief, and it felt good," Leah remarked as he walked her to her car. "I thank you so much. And I have no regrets. You've been wonderful."

Ryan was quiet and then spoke as an understatement, "I've had a very pleasurable day myself. I'm glad you chose to come with me. Maybe in a week or two you'll consider a movie or an Iowa State football game. Something you can think about."

He made no attempt to kiss her goodnight, and for that she was relieved. He promised he would follow her home to her driveway. Then he could drive the miles back to his house.

Leah pondered the day's events as she drove home. She had laughed and thoroughly enjoyed the pleasant hours in Ryan's company. She was sure Logan would have approved.

Before the drive home was completed, Leah's stomach began to feel queasy.

"Small wonder," she mused. *"I'm too old for all that greasy food. We had how many lemonades? At least three. A corn dog, most of a funnel cake with powdered sugar, beef burger, fries. Oh, my gosh. There was the deep fat-fried Twinkie. Thank goodness I just gagged down a bite of that. That should be outlawed. No wonder I feel sick to my stomach,"* she concluded.

Some relief came to her by turning the car's air vents so that the coolness blew directly on her face. She pulled into her garage where Stranger stood waiting as a valet waits for his master. Ryan turned his car around in her drive way, blinked his brights at her, and honked as he headed back to Mission Falls.

Once inside the house, Leah dropped her overnight bag on the floor and poured herself several ounces of Pepto Bismol. Not particularly wanting to lie down in her own bed, she threw a pillow on the love seat in the den. She was still quite nauseated. "I HATE this," she groaned. "Maybe if I just threw up. Maybe if I just got it over with." She lay very quiet, feeling the cool gentle air from the ceiling fan and arguing with herself.

Moving as little as she could, Leah noticed that Stranger had placed himself on his stomach in the middle of the den floor and was carefully studying her. She closed her eyes and tried to sleep. As a wave of nausea swept over her again, she moaned softly. No one was near, so she could afford the luxury of an audible moan.

Sensing a movement near her, she quickly opened her eyes. Stranger had moved to her side, where he proceeded to lick her elbow and laid his head near hers on her pillow.

"Oh, Sweetie Pie," she said softly. "Thank you for your concern. I'm going to be alright. Just pay back for being so stupid today." She reached up and scratched very gently the long snout and the soft hair under his eyes. "I thank you for your caring so much."

In the end, the contest between the antacid and the poor food choices was lost to the poor food choices. No decision was made to eradicate her stomach of its contents. It just happened that way. Afterwards, she returned to her own, and both she and Stranger slept peacefully the rest of the night.

*   *   *   *   *   *

On the Sunday evening at the end of the State Fair, Leah's parents drove to the farm. Although she often stopped by their house after work one or two evenings a week and still had Sunday dinner with them, they didn't make as many trips into the country.

Ted Weeks ventured on to the barn and the barnyard to evaluate the herd. Leah strolled with her mother to the gazebo, where she regaled her with the story of her trip to the State Fair with Ryan James. Grace Weeks observed the smile on her daughter's face and heard the fun in her voice as she talked. *"Finally! The metamorphosis was beginning and was recognizable."*

"It's good to see you coming alive again, Leah. It's good to see you happy again."

"Mom, I still can't get past this feeling of guilt," Leah said. "I have to admit I had such a really fun day at the Fair with Ryan, but I have this nagging feeling I'm cheating on Logan. I know I'm not, but the guilt is still there. How does a person ever get on with his life?"

Leah's mother leaned forward to her daughter and said very softly, "You have to understand that love doesn't divide. It multiplies. I know this isn't the same scenario, but maybe it's the best I can do to explain," she went on. "When your brother Paul was born, I thought he was the most wonderful child ever. I had so much love to give him, and I poured it all over him. Then a couple of years later, I became pregnant again. We were overjoyed to have another baby, but when you came, I didn't have to take any of my love away from Paul to give to you. That love wasn't divided, it multiplied. The love for him remained the same, and there was just as much love to give to you. Then when Jim came along, the love grew a third time. It multiplied again."

Grace paused and looked steadily at her daughter. "Your love for Logan was a wonderful thing, but, Honey, to find someone else someday doesn't mean you'll take any love from Logan. None whatsoever. It just means there will be more to give someone else. And don't you think Logan would want you to go on and grow in your life here?"

Tears puddled at the corners of Leah's eyes as she leaned forward and grabbed the hands of the diminutive lady. Looking into her gentle brown eyes, she squeezed them and said, "You always told me you knew everything. You weren't kidding, were you?"

Mrs. Weeks laughed and sat back against the side of the gazebo. "It's about time you shaped up and listened to me."

Ted interrupted the two as he stepped into the structure and said, "Did I miss out on something? You two look like you've found a way to make chocolate that will cause you to lose weight. Oh, wait a minute. That's a chick thing, isn't it? Good thing I wasn't here."

They all laughed and settled back to engage in Glendale reminiscing. For Leah it was a pleasant evening and one which broke down barriers to move on. All in all, the ending of a very healing day…a very healing week.

.

Chapter Twenty Two

Stranger's Check Up

True to his word, Ryan called in the middle of the following week and asked Leah again if she'd like to attend the Iowa State/Iowa University football game.

"It looks like the game between MY Cyclones and YOUR Hawks will be the third Saturday of next month. Have you cleared your calendar for that game?"

"I haven't been to a college football game in at least a hundred years," she answered excitedly. "Logan and I didn't miss many high school games. Of course, the best games were the ones between Glendale and Mission Falls, although we've taken a few on the snoot the last couple of years. Your new coach has made a lot of difference for your team. But, yes, in response to your question, I don't have anything on my calendar for that Saturday, and if I did, I'd try to change it." Leah hoped her response didn't sound too eager and was actually surprised to feel that she was.

At the end of that conversation, Leah asked about immunizations and a checkup for Stranger.

"I've had Stranger since this last April, and I've done nothing about his shots. Of course, I don't have any records so I guess I don't know what he needs. I don't know if he's ever had any immunizations at all. I'm sure his teeth should be checked at the same time. And, then, there's his toe nails."

"Why don't you bring that canine friend over Friday evening after you're off work? We can give him a check-up and start him on his shots." Then in an attempt to dangle another carrot, he added, "After we've finished that, you and I could grab some dinner at the Mission Bells."

Friday afternoon Leah's doorway was filled once again by the figures of Dana, Marcie, and Polly. She thanked them for their invitation to join them again for another Mission Bells evening. "I've already made plans for the evening, but, hey, I might see you ladies over there."

"Anyone we know?" Marcie asked suspiciously.

Leah smiled and replied, "You all met him a couple of weeks ago when we were there. In fact, Dana, you danced with him.

Dana charged in some surprise, "You're having dinner with Dr. James, the vet?"

Leah tried to turn the invitation into merely a gesture of a friend's kindness. "Well, it's not so much a date as I think he felt guilty that I had to drive that far to get Stranger's shots." Nervously tapping her pen on her desk, she added, "I think maybe he just felt obligated to make my trip not so burdensome to me."

Marcie inserted, "Do you realize how many women in Mission Falls and Glendale would give their eye teeth to have dinner with Dr. James? He's kind of the county stud."

"Girlfriends, please be assured, Dr. Ryan isn't interested in me, and I'm not interested," and she put up the first two fingers of each hand, "in 'going with' him". I'm not interested in going with ANYONE right now...maybe never." She smiled at the three. "It's just dinner at the Missions Bells and shots for my dog. How romantic is that?"

She watched their reaction, Dana's face expressing doubt. To emphasize to the three there was no relationship involved, she said, "I knew Ryan James when we were in high school. He and his buddies would drive over to Glendale, and we used their swimming pool before this town got our own. So, see? He's just a friend. We'll probably see you over there sometime this evening."

After work Leah drove home and changed into fresh jeans and shirt. Stranger had proven to be an obedient and trouble free passenger and loved to go for rides. Tonight she chose to drive Logan's pickup. Stranger sat in the passenger's seat and looked with interest out the windows.

Leah was introduced to the young intern, Benjamin McFall. Since it was well after six o'clock, Ryan's receptionist and his assistant had left for the day. She and Stranger were given a tour of the facilities. Then Ryan thoroughly checked out her four-legged friend and found no problems. He guessed him to be about seven years old with German shepherd and golden lab ancestry. The question of the short legs remained a mystery. Finally, Ryan and his intern took Stranger to an exam room, and Leah dismissed herself. She didn't relish watching Stranger endure his shots. She was into a short article in Reader's Digest when she heard her dog screaming from the back of the building. Dr. James and Benjamin appeared shortly from the back room, grinning and leading Stranger on his black, braided leash.

"Whatever happened?" Leah asked with some suspicion. "I heard him scream. Not once but seven or eight times. What did you do to him?"

Ryan looked at Benjamin, who was still grinning.

"Your dog took his shots like a hero. But the boy doesn't like his toe nails clipped. In fact, he really doesn't want you to mess with his feet at all. Not mean. Just touchy. Sort of ticklish." He handed Leah the leash. "No harm done. He's a great dog."

Crouching beside Stranger, she gently rubbed the top of his head between his ears. "I should have warned them about your ticklish paws, shouldn't I?"

Looking up at the two men, she said, "When I brush him or just pet him, he will hold so still, almost like he's holding his breath, but when I brush the bottoms of his legs, he starts prancing. I suppose he is ticklish, but maybe someone in his past has clipped his nails too short. Anyway, he'll be more comfortable for a while."

Leah stood up, returned the leash to Benjamin, and speaking to Stranger, announced, "We'll be back after a while. You go with the good doctor, Benjamin. I think the run's shaded, so you'll be alright."

Ryan turned to Leah. "If you don't mind, I'm going to clean up. You don't want to know what some animals can do to you in the course of an exam, Stranger excluded, of course. Ben will be here for a while longer, doing some paper work so you're welcome to stay here or you can walk across the street with me to my house while I shower and clean up. Wherever you're most comfortable."

"Thanks, but I think I'll stay here with Ben and finish the article I was reading." The choice was easy, and she felt at ease…and safe.

Fortunately, in most cases men can do the revitalizing thing more quickly than women. She tried hard not to make comparisons when he returned to the clinic to retrieve her, but she noted the length of Ryan's hair was so much longer than Logan's had been. Logan's cropped, sandy brown summer hair style was so different from Ryan's, which was still dark with traces of gray. She had to admit in his crisp, clean western shirt, Levis, and boots, he might fit the bill of the county stud.

Chapter Twenty Three

A Promise Kept

Ryan asked the hostess to seat them on the restaurant side of Mission Bells. They arrived just past prime time, so they were seated right away. Ryan insisted Leah have a glass of wine and ordered hors d'oeuvres. "I do believe juice from the vine would be good for you. How many others have sat so heroically as they heard the screams of their loved ones from the vet's torture chamber? As in getting toenails trimmed? Ouch!"

The red blush suited Leah and, in fact, produced the same effect on her own cheeks. Conversation began lightly with tales of events in the life of a small town veterinarian. Dr. James' ability to make Leah smile had only improved from high school years, and Leah's laughter was savored by both. By the time dinner was finished as well as another glass of wine, she didn't mind when she felt his hand at the small of her back directing her to the side of the restaurant where the small country band was playing. They found a tall table for two in a corner further from the music.

Leah knew she should disperse the effects of the wine and insisted on coffee. She wasn't inebriated by any means, but the wine affected her more profoundly since she seldom drank. Coffee was delivered to their table in brown, heavy mugs, and Leah noticed Ryan watching her and smiling.

"Why are you laughing, Doc?" she asked, blowing into the mug to cool it.

"I think you would be a cheap drunk, wouldn't you?" he grinned. "Two goblets of wine, and now I'm getting you sober enough to drive home. However, listen, if he could reach the pedals, I think that dog of yours could get you back to Glendale."

She smiled, "I'm learning to do what the big girls do."

The band finished a break and began a second set. When they began, "Amarillo by Morning," Ryan said, "Hey, that's George's music. You can't say "no" to a tune like that."

He stood from the table and held out his hand. Leah was hesitant, but only for a minute. "I'd love to, but, Ryan, I haven't danced in forever." Looking down at his feet, she added, "Heck, you're wearing boots. Take your own chances."

She jumped down from the tall stool and walked beside him to the dance floor. "They say dancing is like riding a bike...it all comes back to you. I guess we'll see."

Ryan was an experienced country dancer, not necessarily fancy, but a smooth dancer with a firm lead. The dance ended, and neither made motions to leave the floor. Looking at the band, he said, "Let's see what they play next."

A waltz. Then another two step. And Leah was smiling. Finally a fast tune was played, and Leah said, "Okay, I'm way out of my league now." As he escorted her back to the table, she turned and said, "That was so much fun."

The waitress brought refills of coffee. "That felt so good. I forgot I could do that, but it's so easy to dance with you, even though you're as tall as you are, and I'm as short as I am. How do you do it?"

"Do you remember one night, back in another century, when a bunch of us guys had driven to Glendale to one of your dances? You danced with me, I'm sure you insisted upon it, and you were no taller then than you are now, and you stood on the tops of my shoes, and I danced with you?" He stopped to reflect. "But most of our dancing then was just standing and wiggling around in front of each other."

Leah laughed aloud. "I DO remember that. And, no, I did NOT insist upon dancing with you." Pointing to his head, she added, "You have some static on the line up there."

By the end of the evening, the caffeine's influence had surpassed the influence of the alcohol. The caffeine combined with the laughter.

They returned to Ryan's clinic and retrieved Stranger from his run. Stranger's tail signaled a happy greeting to both.

"I swear, sometimes I think he actually smiles," she said, addressing Ryan. Without attaching his leash, Stranger was free to walk between them to the pickup. He claimed and marked some territory before he jumped into the front seat.

"My evening was totally delightful. Thank you. This time, send me a bill for Stranger's exams and shots and toe nail trimming. You are way too good to me. And by the way, dancing was fun, too. That was first in a long time."

Ryan smiled. "I'll give you a call and make arrangements for the Cyclone/Hawkeye game. Sometimes I tailgate with Ben and his fiancé, and we leave the office in the hands of my receptionist. She can always call one of us if we're needed. That might suit your fancy. What's better than a brat over a portable camp stove in the back of an SUV? And in the meantime, maybe you'd be interested in seeing a movie next weekend. Or dinner again. Or even some more dancing. I think my toes will be healed by then. Not pushing, mind you. Just leaving some doors open."

He held the door open as she climbed into her small truck. Looking around at the darkened sky, he noted, "There's lightning looks like to the Southwest, and the wind's kicking up a little. Forecasts for heavy rains and winds weren't until way after midnight, so I think you'll be alright if you head straight home."

"I'll be fine," she reassured him.

"I can follow you home if you're uneasy," to which she shook her head. "Then call me when you get there so I'll know you're okay." Before he closed the door, he squeezed her hand. "Thank you for coming over. You made it a great Friday night."

The radio was silent as she headed onto the highway. She talked to her good friend, "You seem to like him, too, don't you, Buddy? And he didn't try to kiss me good night. At least not just yet. Maybe soon, though. Thank you for that, Dr. James."

Stranger sat upright and looked out the window though he saw very little except white, long, jagged flashes in the black sky. He was quiet, apparently listening to every word she said. She continued to ramble and make observations.

It became apparent as she neared Glendale that the wind and rain were of storm magnitude. The winds weren't swirling as of a tornado but were straight gusts, trying to push the pickup off the road.

Leah turned off the highway onto the gravel. Windshield wipers were flapping back and forth with gusto. Winds slashed at the large pick up, pushing the back portion off track. Wanting to drive faster to get safely home, she was nevertheless forced to slowdown. Stranger peered forward and out the side windows, seeing objects only when the lightning struck. Thunder was almost a constant rumble with occasional shouts for attention.

The normally five minute drive on the gravel was a ten almost fifteen minute journey of stress. Leah finally found the driveway to the garage but had to by-pass it and drive on to the machine shed, which always housed the farm pickup. She quickly made the decision to not mess with opening the great doors but to let the small truck ride the storm out in the shed's driveway. Sitting on the north side of the building, it was out of the force of some of the wind and blowing debris. She hesitated a few minutes, deliberating whether to stay in the truck or to run quickly to the house. Finally, sensing some let up in the howling theatre, she decided to make a run for it. Leah opened the pick-up door and shouted, "Come on, Stranger. Let's move."

Lightning had not knocked out the electricity as it's prone to do in rural areas. The yard light gave some vision to the path, a path lined with tall trees that had been part of the farm probably since its existence. Stranger ran along the path with Leah close behind, running with her head down to shield her eyes from the pelting rain.

A sudden lightning strike caused both dog and woman to stop. Stranger's hair stood straight from his back. Leah could feel the hair on her arms raise, and she was immediately aware of the strong smell of sulfur. Stranger ran back to her.

"Come on, Buddy. That was way too close," she screamed.

They had only fifteen or twenty yards to go when Leah heard a branch snap above. At the same instant she was knocked off the path and off her feet by the great German shepherd. A huge branch from the tall, tall cottonwood came crashing down on the path. Leah heard a horrible, "YARK, YARK, YARK, YARK," from her devoted pet at the same time she felt the end of the enormous branch hit her legs and back.

Rain beat down on her. "Stranger," she screamed. The light end of the massive limb had hit her, its smaller branches holding her prisoner. She couldn't move from its burden. Smaller limbs covered her upper torso and face.

"Stranger! Stranger!" she screamed. She was scratched and bleeding from all the smaller branches, that mixed with the mud and the pelting rain. Struggling, she pushed the branches away from her face and tried to raise enough to see where Stranger was. Although somewhat subsiding from its earlier intensity, the wind still blew, and the lightning continued to flash, eventually moving farther away. The yard light had been extinguished as a result of the lightning strike. Finally, a distant flash of lightning allowed her to see Stranger's still back and legs under the large segment of the branch. He was lying where she had been running only seconds before.

Leah felt the horrible pain of her heart breaking as it had last October. She lay back in the wet, soggy grass and began to cry. But she gasped when she heard a very audible voice whisper, "I have to go on now, Leah. You're going to be alright." She felt a soft kiss on her eyelids. Then she heard only the dying wind.

She didn't open her eyes, nor did she try. She lay paralyzed. Paralyzed not from the weight of the tree, but paralyzed because of the weight of her broken heart. She realized her best friend was gone. Again.

Chapter Twenty Four

Surviving the Storm

The rain eventually became gentle, and the wind quieted. Leah was quite aware of the pain in her leg, but that was slight compared to the ache in her chest, the awful ache of her heart breaking again. The weight of the cottonwood limb imprisoned her, and she could move only her upper torso. The tree was too heavy to lift, and she finally decided to lie back in the saturated grass and wait. Dawn wouldn't make its appearance for another six hours. Then Simon would be there to check on the cattle.

* * * * * * *

Ryan watched the clouds as best he could through the darkened skies. He checked his patients in the clinic and then walked across the road to his house. He anticipated Leah would call in twenty to twenty five minutes. A half hour had passed, and he decided to call her. There was no answer.

"That lightning really sharpened up there in the south. Wind picked up, too. Don't suppose there's anything to worry about, but Leah should be home by now. Just

makes me a little uneasy," Ryan fussed. *"Think I'll just hop in the truck and drive over there. If lights are on in the house, and there's nothing amiss, I'll just turn around on down the road and head back home. She'll never need to know."*

The trip to Leah's farm house outside of Glendale revealed the passing of a strong storm. As he turned into her driveway, the downed branches proved the storm had made an impact on Leah's farmyard. He drove down the drive past the garage and stopped not far from the Cottonwood. No lights were on in the house or the yard. Jumping out of his truck, he hollered, "Leah, are you here? Leah! Leah!"

The wind was quiet, and he heard a yell, "Help me. I'm under these branches. I'm over here."

Following the echo of her pleas, he found Leah, covered with mud, blood, and branches.

"My God, Girl! You're hurt!" He was pulling on the branches. "Hold still. Let me see if I can get this off you. I don't want to hurt you."

"Ryan, find Stranger. He's down around my feet, and I haven't heard him. Please find him, and see about him" she cried.

Stranger was easily found. He was confined by a much larger portion of the tree trunk, and Ryan, the informed veterinarian, knew there was no need for speed to free him. He turned back to Leah, "He's there, but I can't do anything for him now. Hang on. I think I can pick this up and throw it off you. Then I'll get an ambulance out here. There's no way I'm moving you."

Ryan flipped open his phone and was relieved to see enough bars to make his call.

"Leah, what happened? We didn't get wind like this in Mission Falls. I was so stupid to let you drive off by yourself," he lamented. "It looks like Stranger took the full impact of that branch. It's a miracle you were out of its way."

"Oh, Ryan. Stranger saved my life. He knocked me out of the way or, you're right, I would have been there. Where is he now? Oh, I can't bear losing him now. I can't bear losing him again."

Ryan was puzzled. "What do you mean, 'You can't bear losing him again?' Did you lose him before? Had he run away?"

Leah was silent. "I mean I can't bear the thought of losing him."

EMTs arrived, and Leah was transported to Glendale's hospital. Her leg was x-rayed and displayed a broken Tibia. The break was clean and promptly cast. More examinations indicated kidneys and back muscles were bruised, and the doctor insisted she remain in the hospital through the coming day.

Ted and Grace Weeks met the ambulance at the emergency room, and Merrill and Rachel arrived later as the dawn was appearing. Leah slept some and later took a few practice runs on her crutches. Before lunch Ryan appeared in the doorway. With help, Leah had managed a shower and dressed in clean clothes brought to her by her mother. She had moved to a chair, propping her leg on a footstool. Ryan pulled a chair close to hers.

"Dang," he said. "I was hoping I'd get to see you in one of those charming, backless gowns with the tie at the neck. Didn't make it in time, did I?" He smiled, but not with the big grin that she usually saw.

"I can't tell you how much I've beat myself up," he continued, "that I didn't make you stay at my house until I knew the storms had passed. Why did I let you go out in that?" He looked earnestly at her. "This is Iowa. I know about storms here. I'm so sorry I let you go."

Leah looked at Dr. James with equal seriousness. "Since when did you become the all-knowing meteorologist? I thought animal medicine was your bag. Like you're smart enough that you could divine a lightning strike or a huge wind? And, by the way, we would have been alright if not for either of those; though I'm not sure if the lightning struck the tree and then the wind caught it or just what. Guess I won't know."

She was quiet as her eyes filled with tears. Ryan didn't speak, waiting.

"Where is Stranger? Did you move his body?"

Ryan replied, "After your folks made it here to the hospital, I left and hurried back out to your farm. I had called Merrill and Rachel to let them know what had happened. Here it was, the middle of the night, but I figured they needed to know, too. After I told them you would be okay, Merrill wanted to come right out and see which tree had fallen and to assay any other damage. I met him out there, and even though there was still no light back there since the electricity hadn't come on yet, we turned our truck headlights on the mess. We could see where Stranger was. When I moved the tree branch off you, I had also moved it a little bit off of Stranger, but he was still covered by some of the limbs on it. We moved what was covering him, and Merrill pulled him clear. I had a cover or a big old blanket in the back of my truck, and we wrapped Stranger in that. That's no small dog, you know, but between Merrill and me, we carried him down to the machine shed. We'll do with him whatever you want. "

Leah knew she would never tell anyone of Stranger's death, of the voice, of the kiss. That would always be between Logan and her. She was quiet and swallowed hard to keep the tears from her eyes as they found their way up out of her chest and then past her lips. She looked at Ryan and said very quietly, "There's only one place to bury him. I'll go home this evening, and tomorrow we'll bury him near the big lilac bush next to the gazebo. I hope you can come to my friend's burial."

Ryan smiled and, leaning forward, squeezed her hand. "I'll definitely be there."

ABOUT THE AUTHOR

After leaving home in Centerville, Iowa, Kathryn taught elementary school in a nearby town. She says that teaching second grade was the best--students were mature enough to tie their own shoes and button their own coats but were sweetly unsophisticated enough to make paper hearts for her saying, "I love you, Mrs. Wood." With her husband, Kathryn raised two children, working in various jobs along the way and keeping her family, wide circle of friends, and neighbors entertained with an endless stream of jokes, wisecracks, and often tender, frequently wise, observations on the world and people around her.

Kathryn has a great talent for telling stories and entertaining people, and those of us who hold her dear are thrilled she has finally put some of this talent down on paper (or created it digitally may be the correct way to say it these days) so that many others can enjoy her as well. Kathryn can make you cry with laughter or with the heart-felt realization of a shared sorrow. She is currently retired, living with her totally undisciplined dog, Trooper, who makes her laugh out loud every day.

Made in the USA
Charleston, SC
16 August 2013